MARY NORTON

BONFIRES
AND
BROOMSTICKS

Illustrated by
Anthony Lewis

DENT CHILDREN'S BOOKS
LONDON

For Pickle

This edition published in 1993
Reprinted in 1998
First published in 1947
Text copyright © Mary Norton, 1947 and 1957
Illustrations copyright © Anthony Lewis, 1993

The right of Mary Norton and Anthony Lewis
to be identified as the Author and the Illustrator of this work
has been asserted by them in accordance with the Copyright,
Designs and Patents Act 1988.

Typeset by Deltatype Ltd, Ellesmere Port
Printed in Great Britain
for J. M. Dent by
Butler & Tanner Ltd, Frome and London
The Orion Publishing Group
Orion House
5 Upper St Martin's Lane
London WC2H 9EA

A catalogue record for this book is available from the British Library

CONTENTS

LOST. AND FOUND

There was a knock at the door, and two children, partly dressed, ran headlong down the stairs and into the hall. The girl, who had only to tie the tapes of her blouse, reached the front door first. The boy, struggling into a grey woollen pullover, saw her seize the folded newspaper and run with it into the dining-room. She slammed the dining-room door in his face and held the knob. There was a struggle, a bit of kicking on wood, and a voice from upstairs saying:

'Children! Quiet – please!'

'It's come!' called the boy, pushing against the door with all his weight until it opened slowly. '*The Times* has come with our advertisement!' He put his foot in the crack of the door. 'But Carey won't let me see it.'

'Won't I?' said the girl. She stepped back, suddenly releasing the door, and her brother fell into the room.

'Oh, come on, Carey,' he said in an injured voice. 'I wrote half of it.'

Carey spread out the newspaper on the hearthrug (the

table was laid for breakfast). 'Mother wrote it,' she said.

Both children went down on their knees.

'Look, Charles, look. Personal Column. Here it is.' Carey was practically upside down, her nose almost touching the newsprint. 'Lady,' Carey read aloud, 'engaged in work of national importance seeks summer home for three children, aged eight, eleven, and twelve. Seven guineas weekly, inclusive. Reply Box 0014, *The Times*.' She gazed at the page, drunk with the pride of part authorship. 'It looks lovely,' she said.

Charles moved Carey's plaits which lay snakelike on the paper. 'Let's see some of the others. . . "Pale Hands my heart is singing. Pat" –'

'Singing what?'

'Pat.'

'Pat?'

'Pat's the name. "Mink coat scarcely worn" –'

'Look,' interrupted Carey, 'here's one like ours the other way round: "Lady," ' she read, ' "with small house in country willing accommodate two London children as paying guests. Moderate terms. Highest references. Reply E. Price, Little Alders, Much Frensham, Beds" . . .' Carey's voice, as she went on reading, had grown slower and more hesitating. 'It's –' she stared unbelievingly at the printed words, 'it's – Miss Price,' she said in a strange, almost frightened voice.

Charles leaned over and stared at the paper.

'Little Alders?' he repeated wonderingly. 'Was that the name of the house?'

'I don't remember. But Miss *Price* –'

'There must be heaps of Prices in Much Frensham.'

'But E. Price!' Carey's eyes were open wide. 'Miss Price's name was Eglantine.'

'Was it?' It seemed to Carey that he had become a shade paler.

'Yes. Eglantine Price,' she repeated firmly.

They stared at each other without speaking. Then once more they leaned over the paper.

'It only says two children,' Charles pointed out.

'Oh, Paul can sleep anywhere. If she knew it was us — don't you think?'

'Miss Price . . .' said Charles. He began to smile. 'Carey, just think! Miss Price!'

'I know,' said Carey. Her eyes were shining.

'I never thought we'd see her again, after Aunt Beatrice died.'

'Nor I,' said Carey.

'Mother may not let us go.'

'Oh, but she will. She'd much rather we went to someone we knew.'

'Yes, and she knows Much Frensham through staying with Aunt Beatrice and things. And we could say Miss Price was a friend of Aunt Beatrice's —'

'Well, she was.'

'Not a friend.'

'Yes, she was. Do you remember Aunt Beatrice sending her down some peaches when she fell off her' — Carey hesitated — 'her bicycle?'

'It wasn't a bicycle.'

'I know it wasn't. But we promised not to say. We promised not to tell —'

'Well, we haven't. We haven't even talked about it.'

'We did at first.'

'Not lately, we haven't. And we never did to Paul. You know, Carey —'

'What?'

'Sometimes I've felt as if it were something we'd made up. Like those games you play.'

'Well, it's – it must be over two yers ago now. It is real.' She put her finger on the paper. 'Here's Miss Price again to prove it. It's just that things you can't talk about don't seem real after a bit. I wonder if Paul . . .' She jumped up and ran to the door. 'Paul,' she called, 'come on down.'

Paul came down with his jersey unbuttoned and without a shoe. Carey buttoned up his jersey. 'Where's your other shoe? Oh, never mind. I say, Paul, do you remember Miss Price?'

'Miss Price?'

'Yes. You remember that summer we were staying with Aunt Beatrice? Miss Price was that tall thin lady who had a house near the bottom of the garden, who wore grey coats and skirts and rode on a high bicycle –'

'A high bicycle?'

'Well, higher than they are now. Oh, you must remember her.'

'No, I don't. I don't remember a high bicycle.'

'Oh, you must remember, Paul. Think. It was you who first discovered her.'

'Oh, don't be an ass, Paul,' said Charles. 'You saw her riding a broomstick.'

'Oh, her!' exclaimed Paul. 'Was she Miss Price?'

'Yes, of course she was. And we found her with a sprained ankle that she'd got from falling off the broomstick. And we took her home.'

'And she turned you into a frog.'

'Me?' said Paul, amazed.

'Yes. Only for a few seconds. She was studying to be a witch. You must remember.'

'Oh!' said Paul. 'Did she give us the magic bed?'

'The magic bed-knob. Yes. Now do you remember?'

'Yes. I remember. She had a stuffed crocodile.'

'Yes, and a workroom full of things in jars where she did spells.'

'Yes,' said Paul thoughtfully. 'Miss Price. She was a nice lady.'

'Do you remember why she gave us the magic bed-knob?'

'For fun?' suggested Paul.

'No, it wasn't fun at all. It was to keep us quiet. So we wouldn't tell anyone that she was studying to be a witch. If we told any one, the bed-knob would stop being magic. That's why Charles and I have never talked about it to you. We wanted you to forget.'

'The bed flew,' said Paul.

'Yes, in a way. We had to twist the knob and wish, and the bed would take us to wherever we wanted to go.'

'And you were the only one who could work it.'

'Oh,' said Paul. He began to smile.

'You needn't look like that. It was perfectly easy. It's just that it happened to be your bed-knob.'

'Oh,' said Paul again.

'I mean,' said Carey, irritated, 'that it was off your bed. It was Aunt Beatrice's bed really. You unscrewed the bed-knob.'

'And in my dream,' said Paul slowly, 'we wished to go to prison.'

'Oh, don't be so silly, Paul. It wasn't a dream. We wouldn't all three dream the same dream.'

'Why not?'

'People don't. You each have your own dreams.'

'Did we *really* wish to go to prison?'

'We didn't *wish* to go to prison. We got there by mistake. And it was a police station, not prison. But that's not important. What I wanted know was –'

'And we went to a cannibal island –'

'Yes, but that's not important. What I want to ask you –'

'And the bed got wet –'

'Oh, Paul. Do listen.' Carey gave him a push so that he sat down suddenly in an armchair. She knelt down in front of him. 'Now Paul, do pay attention. The point is this: We are going to stay with Miss Price for the whole summer –'

'In her house?' asked Paul.

'Well, it isn't certain yet,' put in Charles.

'Yes, it's certain. I know we'll go. The question is, Paul,' said Carey, looking very serious, 'what have you done with the bed-knob?'

Paul looked blank.

'You had it,' went on Carey. 'It's been about the house for ages. You had it in your pocket in the train when we were coming home from Much Frensham. I remember saying: "What's the good of a magic bed-knob without a magic bed?" '

'Well, what good is it?' asked Charles.

'It might fit another bed of the same make.'

'Where would you get another bed of the same make?'

'I don't know, Charles,' replied Carey patiently. 'I only ask you, is it sensible or reasonable to go to stay the whole summer with Miss Price without a magic bed-knob?'

'Well, where is it, Paul?' asked Charles, convinced.

Paul's lip trembled. 'I don't know,' he said.

Carey became sterner. 'You must know. Think!'

Paul's face became red. His eyes filled with tears. 'I don't know,' he wailed.

'Shush. Don't make such a row. Come on. Think!'

'I don't know!' roared Paul, trying to escape from the chair. Carey held him by the knees.

'Think!' she insisted.

Paul broke from her grasp with a bellow, and rushed for the door.

At that moment the gong rang for breakfast. Carey got to her feet. 'He can't be trusted with the simplest thing,' she complained bitterly.

Charles was staring at the fire. 'One moment,' he said. He turned to Carey. 'There's somewhere I think I've seen it. Let me think. It was just somewhere the other day –'

'It was in the knife box once,' said Carey.

'No, it wasn't the knife box. It was –'

'I remember thinking, seeing it there in the knife box: "That's the magic bed-knob." I remember thinking Paul ought to have put it away but I wanted a knife quickly –'

'Was it in the tool drawer?' said Charles.

'Yes, but it isn't now. It was in the tool drawer for ages and ages. After they cleaned out the nursery cupboards –'

'I know!' cried Charles suddenly. He ran out of the room and Carey heard him clatter down the basement stairs. Just as Carey was about to follow him the children's mother came down to breakfast.

'What's the matter with Paul?' she asked as she began to serve the porridge.

'Oh, I don't know,' said Carey. 'He'd only got one shoe on.'

Mrs Wilson frowned at the porridge as she shook it from the spoon. 'I think you've been teasing him,' she said.

'He's so silly,' explained Carey.

'So were you, darling, at Paul's age.'

'Oh, Mummy,' exclaimed Carey, scandalized, 'not like Paul! Why, Paul –'

At that Charles thundered up the stairs and burst into the room. There was plaster on his shoulders and his face was beaming. He was rubbing something on his coat sleeve.

'Where was it?' asked Carey, running to him.

'At the back of the broom cupboard, in an old distemper tin.'

'Let me see!'

She held it in her hands. It was splotched with white and rather rusty. She rubbed the white away and saw the old familiar gleam.

'It is it!' she breathed, rubbing harder.

'I saw it the other day,' explained. Charles, 'when I was looking for a piece of old stair rod. I –'

'Children,' exclaimed Mrs Wilson. 'Do come and sit down! Carey, *look* at your hands! What have you got hold of?'

Carey looked up. 'It's nothing, Mummy.' She was almost stuttering with happiness. 'It's just a thing we lost.'

'Well, go and wash your hands and call Paul.'

'Oh, I will, Mummy, I will,' cried Carey warmly.

Charles helped himself to sugar and milk. Then he glanced sideways at his mother. '*The Times* has come,' he observed quietly.

Mrs Wilson felt a little uncertain about Miss Price. There was something odd about all this excitement over a seemingly harmless maiden lady. But to all her questions they gave the most satisfactory answers. Miss Price – quiet, elderly, a little fussy – sounded a most estimable person. Letters were exchanged, and a meeting was arranged. Mrs Wilson, feeling extremely curious, snatched half an hour from her job to have tea with Miss Price at Fuller's. There, over toast and cake, although not able to discover the secret of Miss Price's peculiar charm, Mrs Wilson's fears were laid at rest. Miss Price was just as the children had described her. Reserved but friendly, she expressed a guarded fondness for the children, and her willingness to accommodate all three provided they would be careful with her belongings, and help a little in the house.

'How wonderful . . . how wonderful!' sang Carey, when she heard the news. Even Charles felt impelled to try a hand-stand. Paul looked dubiously from one to another. It was not often their contortions aroused his interest.

'Will we sleep there, Mother?' he asked from the floor.

'Yes, Paul,' said Mrs Wilson in a puzzled voice, 'of course you will sleep there. Why?'

Paul began to smile. It was a slow smile which spread gradually all over his face. He turned away and began plucking at the carpet. 'Oh, nothing,' he said.

Mrs Wilson, as she went upstairs to take off her coat, felt vaguely uneasy.

When they arrived at the station it looked at first as though there was no one to meet them. Then Carey saw the milk-cart on the far side of the level crossing. 'Come on,' she said, 'there's Mr – Bisselthwaite.' She was surprised when the name came so easily to her tongue. Mr Bisselthwaite the milkman . . . of course.

'She ordered an extra two pints,' Mr Bisselthwaite told them, as they climbed on the cart. 'And she said it was you. Growed, hasn't he?' he added, nodding at Paul.

'We all have,' said Carey. The train had gone, and the station was quiet. The grass by the roadside smelt of clover, and high up in the sky a lark sang. 'Oh, it's lovely to be back in the country!'

Clop-clop-clop went the pony. The scent of horse mingled with the scent of fields and deep country stillness spread away on all sides.

'There's Tinker's Hill,' said Charles. Tinker's Hill? How oddly these names came back. And the Roman Remains. 'Look, Paul, that grass-covered sort of wall – that was a

Roman fortress once.'

Paul gazed at the hazy green of the rounded hillside. It seemed to him far away and, at the same time, quite close. It was part of the lovely dream of riding in a milk-cart, part of the clip-clop of the pony's hoofs on the flinty road, part of the rhythmic rise and fall of the dusty piebald back, and the light swift rattle of the wheels.

'Miss Price's house is there, Paul,' said Carey, 'under that hill. You can't see it yet. Oh, you see that lane? That goes to – to Body-something Farm.'

'Lowbody Farm,' said Mr Bisselthwaite.

'Lowbody Farm. Oh, and there's Farr Wood –'

'Look, Paul,' broke in Charles. 'You see those cedars? Those dark trees just beyond the church spire. Well, Aunt Beatrice's house is in there. Where we stayed last time.'

'The Water Board took it over,' said Mr Bisselthwaite.

'Oh,' said Carey. 'When?'

'About a twelvemonth after your aunt died.'

'Oh,' said Carey again. She was silent for a while, trying to imagine the dark old house without Aunt Beatrice; without the high sideboards and the heavy curtains; without the rugs and the tables and the palms in pots; without the . . .

'Mr Bisslethwaite!' she said suddenly.

'Well?'

'Did the Water Board take the furniture?'

'No, the furniture was sold.'

'Who to?'

'Well, there was a sale like. Dealers from London came down. And the village bought a bit. My old woman bought a roll of lino and a couple of chairs.'

'Oh,' said Carey.

So the furniture had been sold. Someone, somewhere, all

AND LOST AGAIN

>unknowing, had bought Paul's bed; was sleeping on it at night; making it in the morning, stripping back the sheets, turning the mattress . . .

'Was everything sold?' Carey asked. 'Beds and all?'

'I reckon so,' said Mr Bisselthwaite. 'The Water Board wouldn't want no beds. Whoa, there,' he called, bringing the pony to a walk. 'Know where you are now?'

It was the Lane – Miss Price's lane that ran along the bottom of Aunt Beatrice's garden. Carey's heart began to beat as she saw a bright cluster of rambler roses among the hawthorns of the hedge, Miss Price's Dorothy Perkins – the ones which twined across her gate. They were thicker, higher, more full of bloom than they had been before. And here was the gate with 'Little Alders' painted on it in white. She glanced at Charles. He too looked slightly nervous.

'Well,' said Mr Bisselthwaite as the pony came to a standstill. 'Here we are. I'll give ye a hand with the bags.'

The gate squeaked a little as they opened it, and the latch clanged. They walked as if in a dream down the straight paved path between the flower beds which led to the front door. It was silly, Carey told herself, to feel afraid.

The door opened before they touched the knocker, and there before them was Miss Price. It was almost a shock. Miss Price – fresh and smiling, and rather flushed. 'I heard the gate,' she explained, taking Carey's bag. 'Well, well, well. This *is* nice! Careful of the step, Paul, it's just been cleaned.' She was as they remembered her, and yet, as people do when you have not seen them for a long time, she seemed somehow different. But something about her long pink nose comforted Carey suddenly. It was a kind nose, a shy nose, a nose which had had a tear on the tip of it once (so long ago it seemed); it was a reassuring nose; it *was* Miss Price.

A delicious smell of hot scones filled the little hall. Miss Price was saying things like: 'Wait a minute while I get my purse. . . Paul, how you've grown. . . Put it down there, Mr Bisselthwaite, please, just by the clock. . . Three and six from ten shillings is . . . Paul, don't touch the barometer, dear. The nail's loose. . . Now let me see . . .'

And then Mr Bisselthwaite was gone, and the front door was closed, and there was tea in the dining-room where the square table took up all the space and the chairs nearly touched the walls. There were scones and jelly and potted meat. And there, through the lace curtain, beyond the window, was Tinker's Hill, steeped rich and gold in the afternoon sunshine, and Carey suddenly felt rested and happy and full of peace.

After tea Miss Price showed them their rooms.

It was a small house, neither old nor new. There were brass stair rods on a Turkey carpet, and at the top of the stairs a picture of 'Cherry Ripe.' Carey's room was very neat, but there were a lot of things stored there as well as the bedroom furniture. Cardboard boxes were stacked on top of the wardrobe, and a dressmaker's dummy, shaped like an hour-glass, stood behind the mahogany towel rack. But there was a little jar of mignonette on the dressing-table, and a spray of dog roses in a vase on the mantel-shelf. Charles's room was neat too – and barer. It had an iron bed and cream-painted furniture. It had probably been a maid's room.

'Paul, I'm afraid,' said Miss Price, 'must sleep on the sofa in my bedroom. You see, I only said two children in my advertisement but' – she smiled round at them quickly, and made a little nervous movement with her bony hands – 'I never thought – I never dreamed it would be you.'

'Weren't you surprised?' asked Carey, coming up to her. They were standing beside Charles's bed.

'Yes, yes, I was surprised. You see, I'm not very fond of strangers. I had to have someone.'

'Why?' asked Paul.

'The rising cost of living,' explained Miss Price vaguely. Then, in a sudden burst of frankness: 'It was putting in the new kitchen sink, really. Stainless steel, you know. And what with the plumbing . . . well, anyway, that's how it was. And, on the whole, I prefer children to adults. Through *The Times*, I thought I might get two well-brought-up ones . . .'

'And you got us,' said Carey.

'Yes,' agreed Miss Price, 'I got you. Had we only known,' she went on brightly, 'we could have done it all without advertising at all. Now you two had better unpack. Where are Paul's things?'

'They're mostly in with Charles's,' said Carey. 'Miss Price.'

'Yes?'

'Could we – could we see over the rest of the house?'

A watchful look came over Miss Price's face. She folded her hands together and glanced down at them.

'You mean the kitchen and the bathroom?'

'I mean –' said Carey. She took a deep breath. 'I mean – your work-room.'

'Yes,' said Paul eagerly, 'could we see the stuffed crocodile?'

Miss Price raised her eyes. There was an odd trembling look around her mouth, but her glance was quite steady.

'There is no stuffed crocodile,' she said.

'Alligator, he means,' put in Charles.

'Nor alligator,' said Miss Price.

There was a moment's embarrassed silence. All three pairs of eyes were fixed on Miss Price's face, which remained tight and stern.

'Oh,' said Carey in a weak voice.

Miss Price cleared her throat. She looked round at them as if making up her mind. 'I think,' she said in a thin kind of voice, 'it would be better if you did see my work-room.' She felt in the pocket of her skirt and brought out a bunch of keys. 'Come along,' she said rather grimly.

Once more, after two long years, they were in the dark passage by the kitchen; once again Miss Price was putting a key in a well-oiled lock and, as if in memory of that other time, Carey's heart began to beat harder and she clasped her hands together as if to stop them trembling.

Miss Price stood aside on the threshold. 'Come in,' she said. 'Go right in.'

The children filed past her and then they stood silent, gazing at the shelves.

'Well?' exclaimed Miss Price sharply. 'It's very nice, isn't it?'

'Yes,' said Carey huskily.

There was no alligator; no chart of the Zodiac; no exercise books; no newts' eyes; no boxes which might have held dried mice. Instead there was row upon row of bottled fruits and vegetables in every shade of colour, from the pale jade of gooseberries to the dusky carmine of pickled cabbage.

Miss Price ran her finger along the labels: 'Tomatoes, apple pulp, plums, greengages, elderberries – they mix very well with black-currants. Do you know that?' 'No,' said Carey, 'I didn't.' 'Red currants, sliced pears, tarragon in vinegar, green tomato chutney. . . What's this? Oh, I know – mushroom ketchup. The label's come off.' She held the jar to the light. 'Looks a bit mottled –' She pushed the jar back out of sight. 'Some of these are last year's,' she explained hastily. 'Red currants, loganberries, and rose-hip cordial.' She rubbed her hands together. 'Well?' she said again, as if waiting for praise.

'It's –' Carey swallowed. 'It's very nice.'

Paul's eyes were round and his face unhappy. 'Where's the crocodile?' he asked bluntly.

Miss Price coloured. 'You see, Paul, I –'

Carey came quickly to her rescue. 'People don't keep things for always, Paul.' She glanced at the shelves. 'Think of the puddings! Think of the lovely, lovely puddings.'

'Yes,' said Paul.

'You see, Paul,' said Miss Price more calmly, 'sometimes

people do things for a bit and then they give them up. Smoking, for instance. People often give up smoking.'

Paul looked bewildered.

'And drink. People give up drink.'

Paul looked still more puzzled. Miss Price smiled at him, very kindly. 'Haven't you ever given up sugar in your tea for Lent?'

Paul blinked his eyes. 'Yes, but –'

'You see, Paul,' interrupted Carey sharply, 'Miss Price has given up alligators. Come on, now.' She began to pull him towards the door.

'For ever?' persisted Paul.

Miss Price nodded her head. 'For ever and ever,' she said.

'Or just for Lent?' put in Paul.

Miss Price glanced at him swiftly. It was a strange look, almost startled: she seemed struck by a sudden idea.

'Lent is over,' she said, but seemed to hesitate. Then once more she became firm. 'No,' she went on. 'For ever and ever. If we do things it shouldn't be by halves.'

'But anything's all right,' said Charles, 'in moderation.'

'Not magic,' said Miss Price.

'You once said even magic.'

'Did I?' asked Miss Price. 'Did I really say that?'

'Yes, you did. I remember quite well.'

'Did I really?' said Miss Price pensively. 'Well. Anyway,' she added quickly, 'come along now. It's nearly Paul's bedtime. Careful of the step.'

Charles wandered out into the garden, while Carey bathed Paul. He leaned over the back fence and stared at Tinker's Hill. So she had given up magic! That was what came of looking forward to something too much – a feeling of flatness and disappointment. Finding the bed-knob, which at the time had almost seemed a 'sign,' now only added to the sense of loss. He thought of Cornwall; and of mackerel-fishing; of rocks and coves and beaches at low tide. Oh, well, he told himself, we're in the country anyway. There would be walks and explorations, and there was always the river. There might even be a boat. And then he felt something move under his shoe. It was a mole, diving upwards through the soft earth and hitting the exact spot where he had placed his foot. In a minute he was on his knees, pulling up the coarse sods of grass which grew down there beside the fence. He dug with his hands into the soft earth, throwing it aside as a dog does, and did not notice Carey until she stood beside him.

'What are you doing?'

'Digging for a mole.' He sat back on his heels. 'I say, Carey –' He looked up at her face and paused. 'What's the matter?'

Carey's expression was odd. She looked half afraid. 'I want you to come and look at something,' she said.

'Let me just finish this!'

'You'll never catch it now.' She paused. 'This is important.'

'What is it?' asked Charles, half getting up.

'Come and see.'

'Can't you tell me what it is?'

Carey turned away and began walking towards the house. Charles followed her. As they reached the front door he said: 'You might tell me –'

Carey turned right round, putting her finger to her lips. 'Ssh –' she said.

'Where's Miss Price?' asked Charles in a loud whisper.

'Ssh –' said Carey again. 'She's in the kitchen. Making macaroni cheese. Come on.'

He followed her up the stairs.

'It's in here,' said Carey, 'where Paul sleeps.' She threw open a door.

It was Miss Price's bedroom. Very clean, very neat, very fragrant. A large photograph of a military gentleman hung over the mantel. There were silver brushes on the dressing-table and a porcelain 'tree' for rings. Paul was tucked up in a bed on the sofa, a small Victorian couch, with a curved back which just fitted him.

'Well, it's all right,' said Charles, staring at Paul, who looked unusually clean and round-eyed.

'What's all right?' asked Carey.

'Paul's bed.'

'I wasn't looking at Paul's bed,' said Carey.

Charles followed the direction of her eyes. Miss Price's bed had a white embroidered spread and a black silk nightdress case lay on the pillow. It was an exciting night-dress case, closely related to a tea-cosy, trimmed with satin blobs like coloured fruit.

'You are dense,' said Carey. 'The bed itself!'

Charles stared.

It was a very ordinary brass bed – a bed like a hundred others. But where at its head there should have been a second bed-knob, the right-hand post ended in a piece of rusty screw.

'Yes,' said Charles. He sat down rather suddenly on the foot of Paul's sofa.

'Is it, do you think?' asked Carey anxiously.

Charles cleared his throat. 'Yes,' he said soberly, 'yes, it must be!'

'There are hundreds of beds like that. She may have had it for years. She may have bought it at the same time as Aunt Beatrice bought hers.'

'Yes,' said Charles. He seemed dazed. 'But the screw. I

think it is. It must be it. She must have bought it at the sale.'
He turned to Carey. 'We can easily tell. Go and get the
bed-knob.'

'That's just it,' said Carey, 'the bed-knob's gone!'

'Gone?'

'Yes. When I'd finished bathing Paul, Miss Price had
done the unpacking. I've been through everything. You can
look yourself. It's gone.'

'She's taken it,' said Charles.

'Yes, she's taken it.'

'Oh gosh!' said Charles. There was a world of disillusion
and sadness in his voice.

Paul lay staring at them glumly over his neatly turned-
down sheet.

Yes, now they were there 'the cupboard was bare'!
Oh, it wasn't that she wasn't glad to see them; it
wasn't that she wasn't very kind and had made up
that lovely bed for Paul on the sofa in her room. It wasn't
that she didn't plan delightful picnics to Pepperinge Eye
and Lowbody Farm, and the Roman Remains; and read to
them at night, and teach them croquet. It was just that she
had given up magic. She seemed to have given up for good
and all. She seemed to have forgotten that she ever knew it.
Right behind the bottled fruits in the larder Paul did once
see some pink and blue which he thought might be the chart
of the Zodiac, but he didn't get a chance to look properly as
the door was nearly always kept locked.

All their excitement, all their planning seemed to have
gone for nothing until one day –

It was Carey's job to put the cleaned shoes by each
person's bed at night all ready for morning. About a week
after they had arrived, when she had forgotten them the
night before, she had to creep down before breakfast to fetch

Paul's shoes from the scullery. As Paul slept on the sofa in Miss Price's room, it meant that Carey had to open that door very very quietly so she could slip in without awaking Miss Price. Well, that was the morning when she found Miss Price's bed had gone.

A faint (the very faintest) film of dust and a pair of quilted slippers marked the place where it had stood. The coverlet was neatly folded on the chest of drawers, and not another thing was out of place. Paul's clothes lay tidily upon his chair, his sofa stood in its usual corner, but Paul himself was nowhere to be seen.

Carey ran down to the passage to call Charles, and he came with her, slowly and sleepily, to see the empty room. They talked it over. They could hardly believe it.

'I told you it was the Bed,' Charles reminded Carey, 'I knew it by that piece of rusty screw.'

'But behind our backs!' exclaimed Carey. 'To have pretended to have given up magic, and then to go and do a thing like this – behind our backs.'

As Carey dressed she grew angrier and angrier. She cleaned her teeth so viciously that she made the gums bleed. She nearly exploded when she heard the bump in Miss Price's room, and Paul's cheerful voice asking if there were raspberries for breakfast.

But barely had she and Charles sat down at table when Miss Price appeared, followed by Paul. Miss Price, looking brisk and neat, and not at all out of the ordinary, went straight to the sideboard to serve the porridge. Paul, who looked as if he had dressed hurriedly, sidled into his place. Except for his unbrushed hair and pullover back to front he, too, looked quite normal. When Miss Price came to the table with the porridge, there was a look of exhilaration about her as if she had had a cold bath. 'A lovely day,' she said

cheerfully as she poured out the coffee. She smiled round the table at the children. 'What are we going to do with it?'

Carey's face became wooden. 'We haven't thought,' she said coldly.

'What about a picnic lunch on the Roman Remains?' suggested Miss Price, undaunted.

'I don't think people should picnic on Roman remains,' said Carey.

Miss Price gave her a curious look, and then she turned to Charles. 'Have you any suggestions, Charles?'

'What is Paul going to do?' asked Charles suspiciously.

Miss Price looked a little taken aback. 'Why, go with you. Unless, perhaps, you go to the Roman Remains. That is a little far –'

'I think,' said Charles, 'we should go somewhere where Paul can come too.'

Miss Price looked surprised. 'Well, of course, that would be nicer. I just thought – that sometimes you and Carey like to do things on your own –'

'No,' said Carey firmly, 'we like Paul with us. Always.'

Miss Price looked really surprised at this. And so did Paul. He sat with his porridge spoon aslant, dripping milk down the front of his jersey.

'Paul!' said Miss Price sharply. Paul came to and swallowed the porridge, and Miss Price wiped off the drips.

'Well, children,' said Miss Price at the end of breakfast, 'you must make your own plans. I have my music lessons, but I shall be free by lunch-time. Go to the bathroom, please, Paul.'

Carey and Charles went out in the garden to wait for Paul. He emerged with a burst almost immediately, his voice raised in a tuneless rendering of 'Hark! the herald angels sing.' Quickly and silently Charles and Carey took him each by an arm and pulled him through the hedge into the meadow. They walked him out of earshot of the house, and then they sat him down in the long grass, still holding him.

'Paul,' said Carey sternly, in a fair imitation of Aunt Beatrice's voice, 'it's no good hedging. Charles and I know all.'

Paul looked bewildered, and tried to pull his arms free.

'You and Miss Price,' went on Carey, 'have been off on the bed. It's no good lying. Charles and I saw.'

Paul looked unperturbed. 'Did you see us go?' he asked.

'Never mind,' said Carey darkly.

Paul, sensing their mood, sat still. He just looked bored, like a pony tied to a stall.

'Well?' said Carey. 'What have you to say?'

It seemed Paul had nothing to say. He fidgeted with his feet, and did not look even interested.

'Have you been often?'

'No,' said Paul, making a not very determined effort to pull his wrist free, 'we were only trying it.'

'Is this the first time you've tried it?'

'Yes.'

'Did it work all right?' asked Charles. He sounded more friendly suddenly.

'Yes.'

Carey let go Paul's wrist. 'Where did you go, Paul?'

Paul smiled.

'Tell us, Paul,' urged Carey, 'we're sure to find out.'

'Guess,' said Paul.

'All right. You must answer "yes" or "no," and you can say "sort of." '

'Was it in the western hemisphere?' asked Charles.

'No,' said Paul.

'Was it the eastern hemisphere?' asked Carey.

'No,' said Paul.

'Then it wasn't in the world!' exclaimed Charles.

'Yes. It was in the world,' said Paul.

'Well then, it must have been in the western or the eastern hemisphere.'

'No,' said Paul. 'It wasn't anywhere like that.'

'He doesn't know what hemisphere means,' Charles suggested.

Paul looked stubborn. 'Yes, I know what it means.'

'What does it mean?'

'Well – it means – It doesn't mean Blowditch.'

'Is that where you went?'

'Yes.'

'You only went as far as Blowditch?'

'Yes.'

'Why, you could walk there,' explained Charles.

'It was only to see if it worked,' exclaimed Paul.

'Did you ask Miss Price if you could try it?'

'No. She asked me. She said: "Let's give it a little twist. I don't suppose it still works." '

'Spells don't wear out,' said Carey.

'How do you know?' asked Charles.

'Well, it stands to reason,' replied Carey.

They were silent awhile. Then Carey said tolerantly: 'I can understand how it happened. But I don't think it's at all fair. And I never have thought it fair that Paul was the only one who could work it.'

'Well, it was his knob,' said Charles. 'We mustn't grumble. There are people who would give anything for a magic bed-knob, whoever had to work it.'

'Yes,' agreed Carey, 'I know. But, as they've had a turn, I think we ought to have a turn too. Miss Price can do as she likes for herself, but *we* never said we'd give up magic.'

'I don't see how we could manage it,' said Charles, 'not with the bed in Miss Price's room.'

Carey tossed back her plaits. 'I shall just go to Miss Price in a straightforward way and ask her right out.'

Charles, slightly awed, was silent.

'And there's another thing,' Carey went on; 'do you remember that when Miss Price gave us the spell she said that if we turned the knob backwards the bed would take us into the past? Well, I think she ought to let us have one go at the past. After that, we could give it up – for a bit,' she added. 'Though I don't see what all this giving up on magic does for anybody. You'd think it might be used for defence or something –'

'Carey!' exclaimed Charles, deeply shocked.

Carey, a little subdued, broke off a stalk of sorrel and chewed it pensively. 'I suppose you're right,' she admitted after a moment. She had sudden visions of dragons breathing fire and mustard gas, and whole armies turning into white mice. It would be terrible, unthinkable, to have one's brother, say, invalided out of the army as a white mouse, kept for the rest of his life in a cage on the drawing-room table. And where would you pin the medals on a mouse?

'You see,' said Charles, 'Miss Price is quite right in some ways. You can overdo things.'

'I know,' Carey admitted. 'But I don't see how it would hurt anybody if we just had a little trip into the past.'

'Well, there's no harm in asking,' said Charles.

They cornered Miss Price after supper. She listened to their argument; she saw the justice of what they said; but she threw up her hands and said: 'Oh dear, oh dear!'

They tried to reassure her; they were very reasonable and very moderate. 'Just one more go, Miss Price, and after that we'll give it up. It's a pity to waste the past.'

'I don't like it,' Miss Price kept saying. 'I don't like it. If you were stuck or anything I couldn't get you out. I've burnt the books.'

'Oh no!' cried Carey aghast.

'Yes, yes, I burnt them,' cried poor Miss Price, 'they were

very confidential.'

'Can't you remember anything by heart?'

'Nothing to speak of. One or two little things. . . Oh dear, this is all my fault. I just wanted to see – out of simple curiosity – if spells wore out. I never dreamed it would start all this up again –'

'Please let us try, Miss Price,' urged Carey. 'Just this once, and we'll never ask again. We did keep our word and you're not really keeping yours if you don't let us just *try* the past. We never told anyone about your being a witch, and now, if you won't let us use the spell again anyway, it wouldn't matter if we did tell –'

'Carey!' exclaimed Miss Price. She stood up. Her eyes gleamed strangely. Her long thin nose suddenly seemed longer and thinner. Her chin looked sharper. Carey drew away, alarmed.

'Oh, Miss Price,' she muttered nervously.

'If I thought –' went on Miss Price, leaning her face closer as Carey backed away. 'If, for a minute, I thought –'

'You needn't think,' Carey agitatedly; 'we wouldn't ever tell. Ever. Because we promised and we like you. But,' she added bravely, 'fair's fair.'

Miss Price stared at Carey a moment or two longer, then, limply, she sat down again in her chair. Her hands lay open on her lap. Tired, she seemed suddenly, and sad. 'Professionally speaking,' she said, 'I'm no good. I should have put a rattling good spell on all three of you, and shut you up once and for all.' She sighed. 'Now it's too late.'

Nervously Carey took Miss Price's limp hand in hers. 'You needn't worry about us,' she said reassuringly, 'you really needn't.'

'And you were wonderful,' exclaimed Charles warmly, 'professionally speaking.'

'Do you really think so?' asked Miss Price uncertainly.

'Yes, Miss Price, we do,' affirmed Carey. 'Don't be discouraged. You'll pick it all up again, easy as pie, once you set your mind to it.'

'You think I will?' asked Miss Price wanly. 'You're not just saying that?'

'I know it,' said Carey, nodding her head.

Miss Price patted her hair as if she felt it had come out of place. 'I hope you're right,' she said, in her usual voice. 'And in the meantime, as you have had some experience, and providing you went somewhere really *educational* and took *every* precaution and were very, *very* careful, I don't see' – she looked at them gravely, almost speculatively, and drew in her breath – 'how *one* little trip into the past could hurt anyone.'

THE 'PAST'

*I*n London, during the reign of King Charles II, there lived a necromancer. (****** These six stars are to give you time to ask what is a necromancer. Now you know, we will go on.) He lived in a little house in Cripplegate in a largish room at the top of a narrow flight of stairs. He was a very nervous man, and disliked the light of day. There were two good reasons for this; I will tell you the first.

When he was a boy he had been apprenticed to another necromancer, an old man from whom he had inherited the business. The old necromancer, in private life, was fat and jolly, but in the presence of his clients he became solemn as an owl, and clothed his fat whiteness in a long dark robe edged with fur, so that he could fill them with respect and awe. Without his smile, and in his long dark robe, he looked as important as a major and as gloomy as a lawyer's clerk.

The young necromancer, whose name was Emelius Jones, worked very hard to learn his trade. It was he who had to turn out at ten to twelve on cold moonlight nights to collect cats from graveyards, and walk the lonely beaches in the grey dawn seeking seven white stones of equal size, wet by the last wave of the neap tide. It was he who had to mash up herbs with pestle and mortar and crawl down drains after rats.

The old necromancer would sit by the fire, with his feet on a footstool, drinking hot sack with a dash of cinnamon, and nod his head saying: 'Well done, my boy, well done. . .'

The young necromancer would work for hours by candle-light, studying the chart of the heavens and learning to read the stars. He would twist the globe on the ebony stand until his brain too rotated on its own axis. On sweltering after-noons he would be sent out to the country on foot to trudge through the fading heather, seeking blind-worms and adders and striped snails. He had to climb belfries after bats,
rob churches for tallow, and blow down glass tubes at green slime till the blood sang in his ears and his eyes bulged.

When the old necromancer was dying he sent for his assistant and said:

'My boy, there is something I should tell you.'

Emelius folded his stained hands in his lap and dropped his tired eyes respectfully. 'Yes, sir,' he murmured.

The old necromancer moved his head so that it fitted more comfortably into the pillow.

'It's about magic,' he said.

'Yes, sir,' replied Emelius soberly.

The old necromancer smiled shyly at the carved ceiling. 'There isn't such a thing.'

Emelius raised a pair of startled eyes. 'You mean –?' he began.

'I mean,' said the old necromancer calmly, 'what I say.'

When Emelius had got over the first sense of shock (he never completely recovered) the old necromancer went on:

'All the same, it's a good paying business. I've kept a wife and five daughters out at Deptford (whence I shall be carried tomorrow), with a carriage and four, fifteen servants, French music teacher, and a bark on the river. Three daughters have married well. I have two sons-in-law at court, and a third in Lombard Street.' He sighed 'Your poor father, may he rest in peace, paid me handsomely for your apprenticeship; if I have been hard on you it is from a sense of duty towards one who is no more. My affairs are in good order, my family well provided for, so the business as it stands and these premises I leave to you.' He folded his hands on his chest and became silent.

'But,' stammered Emelius, 'I know nothing. The love philtres –'

'Coloured water,' said the old necromancer in a tired voice.

'And foretelling the future?'

'Child's play: if you don't go into details, whatever you prophesy about the future comes true sooner or later, and what doesn't come true, they forget. Look solemn, don't clean out the room more than once a year, brush up your Latin, oil the globe so that it spins smoothly – and may good luck attend you.'

That is the first reason why Emelius was a nervous type of man. The second was because in the reign of good King Charles it was still the fashion to send witches, sorcerers, and all those who were reputed to work magic to the gallows, and Emelius, if he made a slip or an enemy, might at any moment be delivered by an unsatisfied client to a very tight and uncomfortable end.

He would have got out of the business if he dared, but all the money of his patrimony had been dispensed in learning magic and he was not a strong enough character to start afresh.

In the year 1666 Emelius, at thirty-five, had become old before his time, old and thin and terribly nervous. He would jump if a mouse squeaked, turn pale at a moonbeam, tremble at his servant's knock.

If he heard a footstep on the stairs he would immediately begin a little spell, something he knew by heart, so that his clients might be impressed as they entered by his practice of magic. He had also to be ready to sit down at the clavichord, in case it was a king's man come to spy upon him, and pretend he was a dreamy musician who had inherited the necromancer's lodging.

One evening, hearing footsteps in the narrow hall below the stairs, he leapt up from the chair where he had been dozing by the fire (these late August nights held the first chill of autumn), trod on the cat (which let out an unearthly squeal), and seized a couple of dried frogs and a bunch of henbane. He lit a wick which floated in a bowl of oil, sprinkled it with yellow powder, so it burned with a blue flame, and hurriedly, with trembling hands, rushed off a little spell – with one eye on the clavichord and the other on the door, and all his body poised for instant flight.

There was a knock, a hesitatingly fumbled knock.

'Who's there?' he called, preparing to blow out the blue flame.

There was a whisper and some shuffling, then a voice, clear and treble as a silver bell, said: 'Three children who are lost.'

Emelius was taken aback. He made a movement towards the clavichord, then he came back to the blue flame. Finally, he stood between the two, with one hand carelessly poised upon the globe, in the other a sheet of music. 'Enter,' he said sombrely.

The door opened and there, thrown into relief against the

dark passageway, stood three children, strangely dressed
and dazzlingly fair. They wore long robes after the style of
the London apprentice, but tied by silken cords, and their
cleanliness, in seventeenth-century London, seemed not of

this world. Their skins shone and Emelius's quivering nostrils detected a delicate fragrance, as of fresh flowers strangely spiced.

Emelius began to tremble. His knees felt unsteady. He wanted to sit down. Instead he looked unbelievingly towards the paraphernalia of his spell. Could two dried frogs and a bunch of henbane do this? He tried to recall the gabble of Latin he had said over them.

'We are lost,' said the female child in that strange foreign voice, clear-cut as rock crystal. 'We saw your light burning, the street door was open, so we came up to ask the way.'

'Where to?' asked Emelius in a trembling voice.

'Anywhere,' said the female child. 'We are quite lost. We don't know where we are.'

Emelius cleared his throat. 'You are in Cripplegate,' he managed to say.

'Cripplegate?' said the female child wonderingly. 'In London?'

'Yes, in London,' whispered Emelius, edging away towards the fire-place. He was terribly afraid. From whence had they come, if they did not know they were in London?

The elder male child took a step forward. 'Excuse me,' he said, very civilly, 'could you possibly tell us what century we are in?'

Emelius threw up trembling hands before his face, as if to ward off the sight of them. 'Go back, go back,' he implored, in a voice broken by emotion, 'from whence you came.'

The female child turned pink and blinked her eyelids. She looked round the dim and cluttered room, with its yellowing parchments, its glass vials, the skull on the table, and the candle-lit clavichord.

'I'm sorry,' she said, 'if we are disturbing you.'

Emelius ran to the table. He picked up the bowl with oil,

the two frogs, the twisted henbane, and with an oath he threw them on the fire. They spluttered, then flared up. Emelius rubbed his fingers together as he watched the blaze, as if to rid them of some impurity. Then he turned, and again his eyes widened so that the whites showed. He stared at the children.

'Still here?' he exclaimed hoarsely.

The female child blinked her eyes faster. 'We will go at once,' she said, 'if you would just tell us first what year it is –'

'The 27th day of August, in the year of Our Lord 1666.'

'1666,' repeated the elder male child. 'King Charles the Second –'

'The Fire of London will take place in a week's time,' said the girl child brightly, as if she were pleased.

The elder male child's face lit up too.

'Cripplegate?' he said excitedly. 'This house may be burnt. It will start at the king's baker's in Pudding Lane, and go on down Fish Street –'

Emelius suddenly fell on his knees. He clasped his hands together. His face was anguished. 'I implore you,' he cried, 'go, go . . . go. . .'

The girl child looked at him. Suddenly she smiled, with kindness, as if she understood his fear. 'We won't harm you,' she said, coming towards him. 'We're only children – feel my hand.'

She laid her hand on Emelius's clasped ones. It was warm and soft and human. 'We're only children –' she repeated. 'Out of the future,' she added. She smiled at her companions as if she had said something clever.

'Yes,' said the elder boy, looking pleased and rather surprised. 'That's what we are, just children out of the future.'

'Is that all?' said Emelius weakly. He got to his feet. He

spoke rather bitterly. He felt very shaken.

Now the youngest child stepped forward. He had a face like an angel with dark gold hair above a white brow. 'Could I see your stuffed alligator?' he asked politely.

Emelius unhooked the stuffed alligator from the ceiling and laid it on the table without a word. Then he sat down in the chair by the fire. He was shivering a little as if with cold. 'What else is about to come upon us,' he asked gloomily, 'besides the fire which will burn this house?'

The little girl sat down on a footstool opposite him. 'We're not awfully good at history,' she said in her strange way. 'But I think your king gets executed.'

'That was Charles I,' the elder boy pointed out

'Oh yes,' said the little girl. 'I'm sorry. We could go back and look it all up.'

'Do not give yourselves this trouble,' said Emelius glumly.

There was a short silence. The little girl broke it.

'Have you had the plague?' she asked conversationally.

Emelius shuddered. 'No – thanks be to a merciful Providence.'

'Good show,' exclaimed the elder boy heartily.

The little girl, asking permission, poked the fire to a brighter blaze. Emelius threw on another log. He stared miserably at the broken bowl blackened by burning oil. The old necromancer had doubly deceived him, for he, Emelius, quite by accident, had found a spell that worked. These children seemed comparatively harmless, but another mixture, lightly thrown together in the same irresponsible way, might produce anything – from a herd of hobgoblins to Old Nick himself.

And it wasn't as if he knew the antidotes. Whatever came would come to stay. He would never feel safe again. Never

more would he dare throw sulphur on the fire with muttered
imprecations; never more would he dare boil soups of frogs'
spawn and digitalis; never more reel off Latin curses or spin
the globe of the heavens into a dizzy whirl of prophecy. His
uncertainty would manifest itself before his clients. His
practice would fall off. His victims might turn against him.
Then he would have to fly, to hide in some filthy hovel or
rat-infested cellar, or it might mean prison, the pillory, the
horse-pond, or the rope.

Emelius groaned and dropped his head into his hands.

'Don't you feel well?' asked the little girl kindly.

Emelius kicked the log farther into the blaze. Then he
raised haggard eyes to the little girl's gentle face.

'A child . . .' he said wonderingly. 'I never knew' – he
dropped his voice sadly – 'what it was to be a child.'

'Oh, you must have known!' exclaimed the elder boy
reasonably.

'Did you always live in the town?' asked the little girl.

'No,' said Emelius, 'I lived in the country. I should have
said,' he went on, adventuring into truth, 'that I had
forgotten what it was to be a child.'

'Well, you're pretty old,' remarked the elder boy con-
solingly.

Emelius looked stung. 'Thirty-five summers!' he exclaimed.

'Have you had a sad life?' asked the little girl.

Emelius raised his eyes. A sad life. 'Ah,' he thought to
himself, 'that's what it is – I have had a sad life.' Suddenly he
longed to tell of his life. The years of fruitless labour, the
dangers of his profession, its loneliness. He could talk with
safety to these strange children who (if he managed to hit on
the right spell) would disappear again into the future. He
pulled his fur-trimmed robe up over his knees away from the

fire, showing coarse yellow stockings which hung upon his legs in wrinkles.

'There are few lives,' he began, rather gloomily but as if he might be going to warm up later, 'sadder than mine. . .'

Then, in quaint words and phrases, he told the children of his childhood, the childhood he said he had forgotten; of how he had been sent out, at an early age, to gather herbs and simples; of the old schoolmaster who had taught him; of May and Maying; of a man who had stood in the stocks for poaching; of being beaten for stealing sugared plums; of how he had hated the nine times table and had worn a dunce's cap for Latin. Then he went on to his apprenticeship in London, the hardships and the disillusionment; the fear of starting on his own, of the terror in which he lived; and of the people who wouldn't pay their bills.

As the children listened the candles grew long shrouds of wax and the fire died low. So absorbed were they in the story that they did not hear the watchman cry the hours nor note the presence of dawn behind the curtain.

'Yes,' concluded Emelius, with a sigh, 'my father's ambition was his son's undoing. In truth I have amassed some small store of gold, but would I had remained a simple horse-doctor in the vale of Pepperinge Eye.'

'Of Pepperinge Eye,' exclaimed the little girl. 'That's close to where we're staying.'

'In Bedfordshire,' said Emelius, his gaze still caught up in the past.

'Yes. Near Much Frensham.'

'Much Frensham,' said Emelius. 'Market day at Much Frensham . . . then were great doings!'

'There are still,' said the little girl excitedly. 'I dare say there are lots of new houses, but the main road doesn't go through there, so it isn't much changed.'

They began to exchange impressions. Emelius it seemed had bathed in their brook, Lowbody Farm had still been called Lowbody Farm; 'a fine new residence' Emelius called it, and he, too, had roamed the short grass on the tiered mound known as Roman Remains.

'Five of the clock,' called the watchman, as he passed below the window, 'and a fine, clear, windy morning.'

They drew back the curtains. The dim room shrank from the clear light and dust danced golden in the sunbeams.

'I wish you could go back to Pepperinge Eye,' cried the little girl. 'I wish you could see it as it is now.'

Then they, in their turn, told him of their lives and of the magic bed. They told him how they had left the bed a few yards down the road in a walled churchyard. It was then they remembered the string bag, tied fast to the bed-rail, with the cheese sandwiches, and the thermos of hot cocoa. Emelius, his housekeeper being still 'abed,' was much put to it to find food, but at length he produced from the larder two legs of cold roast hare and a jug of beer. He was deeply relieved to hear that it was no spell of his which had called these children from the mysteries of the future, and was more than anxious to go with them to the churchyard so that he might see the bed.

They set out, a strange procession, Emelius carrying the jug of beer with the hare wrapped neatly in a napkin. The yard gate was open and there, behind the biggest tomb, they found the bed just as they had left it, with the string bag tied securely to the foot.

It was there they had their early breakfast, while the hungry cats prowled around, and the city slowly woke to the clang and rumble of a seventeenth-century day. And it was there, without mentioning her name, that they told about Miss Price.

A VISITOR

M iss Price slept in Carey's room the night the children were away. She had a restless night. She was not feeling at all happy about having let them go off on their own. She had been caught between two sets of fairnesses. What was fair, she thought, to the children was hardly fair to their parents. Besides, a trip into the past could not be planned with any degree of accuracy. They had seen first how many twists the bed-knob allowed, and then they had made a rough calculation of period. They had aimed for the time of Queen Elizabeth, but goodness knew what they had got. Charles rather cleverly had made a scratch with a pin, from the side of the knob, across the crack, and down the base of the screw. And when Paul twisted he was supposed to twist until the two ends of the scratch met evenly. All very rough and ready, as neither Miss Price nor the children knew if the period covered by the bed-knob embraced the beginning of the world or just the history of England from 1066 onwards. They had assumed the latter.

'Oh dear,' muttered Miss Price to herself, tossing and turning in Carey's bed. 'If they come back safe from this trip it will be the last, the very last I shall allow.'

She had tried to be careful and to make all sensible precautions. The bedclothes had been carefully folded and put away and the mattress covered by a waterproof groundsheet. She had provided the children with a thermos of hot cocoa, bread and cheese, and a couple of hard-boiled eggs. She had given them an atlas and a pocket first-aid kit. Should she have furnished them with a weapon? But what? She had no weapon in the house barring the poker and her father's sword.

'Oh dear,' she muttered again, pulling the bedclothes round her head as if to shut out a persistent picture of the children timidly wandering through a bleak and savage England inhabited by *Diplodocus carnegii* and sabre-toothed tigers. And that Neanderthal man, she told herself unhappily, would be utterly useless in an emergency. . .

Towards morning she fell into a heavy sleep, and was awakened by the sudden opening of the bedroom door. The bright sunshine streamed in through the partially drawn curtains, and there, at the foot of her bed, stood Carey.

'What time is it?' asked Miss Price, sitting bolt upright.

'It's nearly nine o'clock. The boys are dressed. I didn't like to wake you –'

'Thank heaven you're back safely!' exclaimed Miss Price. 'You can tell me all your adventures later. Is breakfast ready?'

'Yes, and the boys have started. But –' Carey hesitated.

Miss Price, who had put her feet out of bed, and was

fumbling for her slippers, looked up.

'But what?'

'We've got to lay another place,' said Carey uncomfortably.

'Another place?'

'Yes – I, we – You see, we brought someone home with us.'

'You brought someone home?' said Miss Price slowly.

'Yes – we thought you wouldn't mind. Just for the day. He needn't stay the night or anything.' Carey's eyes seemed to plead with Miss Price. She grew pinker and pinker.

'He?' repeated Miss Price.

'Yes. His name is Emelius Jones. Mr Jones. He's a necromancer. He's awfully nice, really, underneath.'

'Mr Jones,' echoed Miss Price. She hadn't had a man staying in the house since her father died, and that was more years ago then she cared to remember. She had forgotten all their ways, what things they liked to eat and what subjects they liked to talk about.

'What did you say he was?' asked Miss Price.

'He's just a necromancer. We thought you wouldn't mind. He lived near here once, with an aunt. We thought you'd have a lot in common.'

'Who's going to take him back?' asked Miss Price. She frowned. 'No, Carey, I do think this is thoughtless of you. I had made up my mind this was the last trip the bed was going to make and there you go picking up strange necromancers who you know perfectly well have to be taken home again, which means another journey.' She pushed her feet into her bedroom slippers. 'Where did you say he was?'

'He's in your bedroom,' said Carey. 'On the bed.'

Miss Price looked really put out. 'Oh dear,' she said. 'Whatever next?' She slipped her arms into her blue flannel dressing-gown. 'How am I to get my clothes, or do my hair, or anything? I really am annoyed, Carey!' She gave a vicious tug as she tied up her dressing-gown. 'You must take him down to breakfast, and I'll have to see about him later.'

Emelius meekly followed Carey down the stairs. He looked dazed and gazed wanly about him. As he took his place at the breakfast table, he staggered slightly against Paul, who was half-way through his porridge.

Carey looked worried. 'Mr Jones, are you all right?'

'Yes, I am well enough.'

'You look so pale.'

Emelius ran a limp hand across his wind-blown hair. 'Small wonder,' he remarked, smiling faintly.

Carey gazed at him uneasily; she was thinking of Miss Price; would he, she began to wonder, give the right kind of impression? In the bright light of day Emelius looked far from clean: his tousled hair hung wispily about his ears and his pallid skin was greyish. The long thin hands were stained, she noticed, and the nails were rimmed with black. The velvet of his fur-trimmed robe, though rich, was sadly spattered; and when he moved he smelled of cottage kitchens.

There was no time to do anything about it, however: Miss Price came in almost immediately, looking slightly flustered. She was wearing her best pink blouse, the one she kept for trips to London. Emelius rose to his feet – long and thin, he towered above the table.

Miss Price, in one swift glance, took in his appearance. 'So this is Mr Jones?' she remarked brightly – not, it seemed, to anyone in particular.

'Emelius Jones. Your servant, Madam. Nay' – he bowed deeply – 'your slave –'

'How do you do,' put in Miss Price quickly.

'– humbly content,' Emelius persisted, 'to raise his eyes to one whose subtle craft maturing slowly through the ages as a plant in the dark earth spreads its roots and sucks its sustenance bringing forth shoot and stem and branching foliage to burst at length into dazzling blossom blinding in this your twentieth century the reverent gaze of one who dared to doubt . . .'

Miss Price, blushing slightly, moved to her place behind the teapot. 'Oh well,' she exclaimed, and gave a little laugh, 'I wouldn't say that exactly. Do you take milk and sugar?'

'You are bountiful,' exclaimed Emelius, gazing at her spellbound.

'Not at all. Do sit down.'

Emelius sat down slowly, still gazing. Miss Price, her lips pursed, poured out two cups of tea in thoughtful silence. As she passed his cup, she said conversationally: 'I hear you have an aunt in these parts.'

'And a house,' put in Carey quickly – to establish Emelius as a man of property might help, in Miss Price's eyes, she felt, to enhance his status. 'At least, it will be his. On Tinker's Hill . . .'

'Really?' remarked Miss Price. She sounded dubious. She helped herself to a boiled egg and began to tap it thoughtfully. 'Is there a house on Tinker's Hill?'

'Yes, indeed,' Emelius assured her, 'a comely, neat house – with an apple orchard.'

Miss Price looked non-committal. 'Really?' she said again, then, remembering her manners: 'Porridge, corn flakes, or rice crispies?'

He took porridge. Again there was silence – only comparative: Emelius was a noisy eater and not, Carey noticed, a very tidy one. When he drank down his tea in a series of gulps (as though it were medicine, thought Carey), Miss

Price tightened her lips and glanced at Paul. 'You had better get down, dear,' she said.

'I haven't finished,' complained Paul.

'Eat up, then. Quickly.'

Paul, nothing loath, gobbled noisily, copying Emelius. Miss Price, averting her face, took a dainty spoonful of boiled egg which, closing her eyes, she consumed very slowly. 'Oh dear,' thought Carey, who knew this sign. She glanced sideways at Emelius, who, having peeled one egg and eaten it whole, was reaching for another. He picked off the shell abstractedly, deep in thought. Suddenly he gave a large belch.

Miss Price opened her eyes but she did not change her expression. 'Some more tea, Mr Jones?' she asked sweetly.

Emelius looked up. 'Nay, I am well enough,' and, as he thought they seemed puzzled, he added quickly, 'but 'tis an excellent infusion. None better. And good they say against the Falling Sickness.'

'Really?' said Miss Price again, and hesitated. 'Some toast and marmalade?'

'Marmalade?'

'It's a preserve made from oranges.'

'Ah yes, indeed,' exclaimed Emelius, 'I am very partial to it.' He took the cut-glass dish and, using the jam-spoon, quite unhurriedly he scraped it clean. Paul was fascinated: his eyes seemed to bulge and his mouth fell open.

'Now, get down, Paul,' Miss Price said quickly when he seemed about to speak; and she turned again politely to Emelius, who, more relaxed, was leaning back in his chair thoughtfully licking the jam-spoon. 'The children tell me you are interested in magic?'

He laid down the spoon at once, all courteous attention. 'Yes, that is so. It is, as one might say, my calling.'

'You practise for money?'

Emelius smiled, shrugging slightly. 'For what else?'

Miss Price, quite suddenly, looked pleasantly flustered. 'I don't know . . . You see –' Her face became quite pink. 'A real professional! I've never actually met one . . .'

'No?'

'No.' Miss Price hesitated, her hands clasped together in her lap. 'You see . . . I mean . . .' she took a long breath, 'this is quite an occasion.'

Emelius stared. 'But you, Madam – do you not practise for money?'

'I? Oh dear me, no.' She began to pour a second cup of tea. 'I'm only an amateur – the merest beginner.'

'The merest beginner . . .' repeated Emelius, amazed. He stared even harder. 'Then – if I understand rightly – it was not you, Madam, who caused the bed to fly?'

'The bed-knob? Yes, that was me. But' – she laughed a little deprecatingly, sipping her tea – 'it was quite easy really – I just went by the book.'

'You just went by the book,' repeated Emelius in a stunned voice. He drew out an ivory toothpick and, in a worried way, began to pick his teeth.

'Yes.' (Carey felt happier: now Miss Price was almost prattling.) 'I have to measure everything. I can't do a thing out of my head. I'd very much like to *invent* a spell. That would be so worthwhile, don't you think? But somehow . . .' She shrugged. 'You, I dare say,' she went on, dropping her voice respectfully, 'have invented many?'

For one panic-stricken moment Emelius caught Carey's eye. He quickly looked away again. 'No, no –' he declaimed, then, seeing Miss Price's expression, he added modestly, 'none to speak of.' He gazed in a hunted way about the room and saw the cottage piano. 'That's a strange instrument,' he

remarked quickly, as though to change the subject.

Miss Price got up and went towards it. 'Not really,' she explained, 'it's a Bluethner.' As Emelius came beside her, she raised the lid of the keyboard. 'Do you play?'

'A little.'

He sat down on the music stool and struck a few notes,

half closing his eyes as though listening to the tone. Then, head nodding and fingers skipping, he swept into a little piece by William Byrd. He played with great feeling and masterly restraint, using the piano as though it were a harpsichord. Miss Price seemed quite impressed.

'That was very nice,' she admitted guardedly. And, glancing quickly at her watch, she moved away and began to clear the table.

'It was lovely,' cried Carey warmly, as she jumped up to help; 'do play some more!'

Emelius, turning to look at her, smiled a trifle wanly. 'Saepe labat equus defessus,' he explained, glancing at Miss Price.

Miss Price looked back at him, her face expressionless. 'Yes, quite,' she agreed uncertainly.

'Or perhaps,' Emelius went on, 'one might more truly say "mira nimia oculos inebriant"?'

'Well,' said Miss Price, and gave a little laugh, 'it's as you like, really,' and she clashed the plates together rather noisily as though to make a distraction.

'I think,' said Charles uncertainly, aside to Miss Price, 'that perhaps he means he's tired . . .'

Miss Price blushed warmly, immediately all concern. 'Oh dear, oh dear . . . of course: how stupid of me! Charles, dear, put a chair under the mulberry-tree for Mr Jones: he can rest there quietly . . .' She glanced about the room. 'And we must find him something to read. Where's the *Daily Telegraph*?'

They could not find the *Telegraph*, but found instead a book called *Little Arthur's History of England*. 'Couldn't he have this?' Charles urged. 'It would be even better. I mean, it would be all news to Mr Jones from chapter seven onwards?'

They went out through the back way, for Emelius to see the kitchen. Surprised and delighted, he admired all the right things in the right way – the electric cooker, the plastic plate-rack, and the stainless steel sink. He clothed his wonder in odd, poetical phrases. Miss Price seemed very pleased. 'I can't afford a refrigerator – at least, not yet,' she told him as she ran a loving hand across the gleaming surface of the sink. 'But this is rather jolly, don't you think? Forty-three pounds seven shillings and tenpence, excluding the plumbing. But worth it in the end, wouldn't you say?'

But it was in the garden that Emelius came into his own. His knowledge of plants astounded even Miss Price, and he told her countless uses for what had seemed the commonest of herbs. Mr Bisselthwaite's boy, who was delivering the milk, broke off his whistling to stare at Emelius. Emelius, his long velvet robe sweeping the lawn, returned the milkboy's stare with sombre dignity. The whistling was resumed, and the milkboy clanged down the two pints with his usual roughness.

Later, leaving Emelius with a history book in the shade of the mulberry-tree, reading with much interest of what was to come to pass in his future, Charles and Carey sought out Miss Price in her bedroom.

'Miss Price,' whispered Carey, as if Emelius might hear, 'do you like him?'

Miss Price, who was making up the bed, paused, sheet in hand. 'He has distinction,' she admitted guardedly.

'Think, Miss Price,' went on Carey, 'of the things you'd have to talk about. You haven't even begun –'

Miss Price wrinkled her forehead. 'Ye-s,' she said uncertainly.

'It's the opportunity of a lifetime,' Charles pointed out.

Miss Price turned. She sat down suddenly on the edge of

the bed. 'I had better be perfectly frank,' she announced firmly. 'He could only stay on one condition.'

'What condition?' they asked excitedly.

The tip of Miss Price's nose became rather pink.

'He must be persuaded to have a good hot bath, and he must have a hair-cut.'

'Oh, I'm sure he'd do it. Willingly,' said Carey.

'And his clothes must go to the cleaners.'

'But what will he wear meantime?'

Miss Price looked thoughtful. 'There's that old Norfolk suit of my father's, and . . . yes, I've some things in a trunk . . .'

Carey and Miss Price were not present when Charles tackled Emelius under the mulberry-tree, but in the still summer air the sound of their voices floated in through the open window. Charles's voice was a burbling monotone, but Emelius's was raised. The conversation went on and on. There were a few deep silences. Carey shut her eyes and crossed her thumbs: the going, she realized, was not easy. At last, through the mist of leaves, she saw Emelius stand up. As the two figures began to approach the house, Carey drew back into the room, but not before she heard Emelius's parting shot, delivered in a voice which broke. 'So be it,' he said, 'if it is the custom, but I had an uncle died of the ague through this same cause.'

Preparing Emelius's bath was something of a ceremony. Miss Price dug out her fluffiest and softest bath-towel, and a clean cotton kimono with an embroidered spray of flowers across the back. Carey ran the water to a pleasant, even temperature, and threw in a handful of bath salts. She spread out the bath-mat and closed the window. Emelius was ushered in, the plumbing was explained to him by

Charles, and he was asked to put his clothes outside the door.

He was a long time in the bath. The children tiptoed around the house in a state of nervous anxiety, as if a major operation was taking place upstairs.

After a while, they heard him running the hot and cold taps, and raise his voice, against the sound of the water, in a little Shakespearian ditty, slightly off the key.

'He's enjoying it,' said Charles.

Emelius bathed, his soft mouse-coloured hair falling carelessly across his brow, looked almost ten years younger. And there was an old-fashioned distinction about the Norfolk suit. It fitted him quite well: Miss Price's father, Carey realized, must have been as thin and angular as Miss Price. The buckled shoes, perhaps, were not quite right, but the over-all affect was pleasing: he looked rather romantic, or – as Charles put it – 'like some kind of poet from Oxford.'

Miss Price examined him with critical eyes and, on the whole, seemed pleased. With comb and nail-scissors, she lightly trimmed the hair behind his ears. 'That's better,' she said, as she brushed him down – modestly proud, she seemed, as though she had invented him. 'Now let me see your nails . . .'

Emelius submitted humbly to being turned about; to having his tie knotted and his collar straightened: this was his homage to a master-craftswoman – one who would always know best.

They arranged to make tea a picnic meal, and to take Emelius across the fields to Pepperinge Eye. It was with no small excitement that they started out on this expedition. Miss Price herself looked strangely moved as Emelius with sparkling eyes named each field or wood. There were few changes. Rush Field, Stummets, Cankerho, these had been the same in his day. Blowditch in Emelius's time had been called Bloodyditch, an echo of past battles, but Farr Wood was still Farr Wood, 'and still,' said Carey, who had walked there often, 'as far.' Emelius could not find his father's house in Pepperinge Eye. He thought it had stood on the site of the present vicarage. They all insisted upon going into the churchyard to see if, by any chance, Emelius had been buried there. But he wasn't – at least he couldn't find his own grave. He found, however, the grave of his aunt – Sarah Ann Hobday – and to his surprise, after scraping the lichen from the nearly defaced gravestone, he found that she died on 27th August 1666, the day – was it yesterday? – on which the children had appeared in his rooms.

It was like getting a telegram.

'Oh dear,' said Miss Price, distressed. 'I am so sorry. Perhaps we had better go home . . .'

'Nay,' said Emelius sombrely. 'Charon waits for all. Better to live well than to live long. I had not seen her since I was a child . . .' He sighed. 'Every light has its shadow.'

'And it's an ill wind –' began Charles eagerly.

Miss Price turned sharply. 'What can you mean, Charles?'

'Nothing,' said Charles. He looked a little shamefaced and stooped to pick up a stone.

'He's thinking of the house,' said Carey. 'Couldn't we go and see it?'

'Well, really, Carey –' began Miss Price; she seemed a little shocked.

'I mean, as we're so near? What's the good of going home? We'd only sit and mope. It might cheer him up,' she added quickly, 'I mean, it's his house now . . .'

'Would it yet be there?' asked Emelius.

Miss Price looked thoughtful. 'I don't see why it shouldn't be.' She turned to Emelius. 'Do you know the way?'

Yes, he knew the way all right – none better – by Tinker's Lane. But this they found had become a cart track and disappeared into a farm. TRESPASSERS WILL BE PROSECUTED said a notice on the gate and a large black dog rushed out to bark at them.

'No matter,' Emelius told them. Suddenly taking the lead, he led them back to the road and, skirting the farm buildings, he took them through fields and spinneys to the base of the hill beyond. Miss Price became a little fussed and dishevelled – climbing through hedges was not her forte. 'Are you sure there isn't a bull?' she would ask, perched precariously on the upper rungs of a five-barred gate.

At last they found the track again – a faint depression in the turfy grass. No more hedges: the hill swelled steeply above them. There was chalk and harebells and an occasional clump of beech-trees. They followed the curve of the hill until at last the view widened beneath them and a sweet breeze stole their breath. Carey found a fossil, Miss Price mislaid a glove.

While they were searching, Emelius went ahead; turning a sudden corner he seemed to disappear. When at last they came upon him, he was standing in a hollow, knee-deep in brambles. Among the brambles there were stones and rubble. It might well have been the ruin of a house, Carey thought – looking about her – awash with elder-bushes and trailing honeysuckle. Tears of disappointment came to her eyes. 'Was it really here?' she asked, hoping he might be mistaken.

'Indeed, yes,' Emelius assured her. He seemed elated rather than depressed – as though this was proof of his having skipped the centuries. He took Miss Price's hand

and helped her down – quite excited he had become, almost boyish – and left her marooned on a piece of coping while gingerly he jumped from stone to stone showing the general lay-out of the rooms. 'Here was the parlour, here the dairy. This,' he exclaimed as he jumped down into a long hollow, 'was the sunken garden where my aunt grew sweet herbs.' He kicked the sandy rubble from some flat stones. 'And here the cellar steps.' He showed them where the apple orchard had been, and the barn. 'It was a comely neat house,' he repeated proudly. 'And none to inherit it save I.'

When they reached the main road a strange incident occurred. Emelius disappeared. One moment he was walking just behind them, and the next he was nowhere to be seen. Miss Price stopped Dr Lamond in his old Ford and asked him if he had seen, along the road, a young man of Emelius's description.

'Yes,' said the doctor. 'As I turned the corner he was close behind you, then he made a dart for that field.'

They found Emelius behind the hedge, white and shaking. It was the car which had unnerved him. His panic, in the face of such a monster, had left no place for courtesy. It was some time before Miss Price could calm him. When the mail-van passed them later Emelius stood his ground, but the sweat broke on his brow, and he quivered like a horse about to shy. He did not speak again until they reached home.

MAGIC IN MODERATION

Breaking Emelius into twentieth-century life was not easy, but Miss Price had great patience. He learned to clean his own shoes, and to pass the bread and butter at tea. He became more modern in his speech, and once was heard to say O.K. They had no sooner got him used to cars when he saw a jeep, and all their good work was undone. Aeroplanes he marvelled at, but they did not come close enough to frighten him. But daily, as he learned more of the state of the world, modern inventions, and the march of progress, he clung closer to Miss Price as the one unassailable force in the midst of nightmarish havoc.

On warm evenings, after the children were in bed, he would be with Miss Price in the garden, stripping damsons with a rake (for bottling), and they would talk about magic. Carey could hear them through her window, their voices rising and falling in restrained but earnest argument as the damsons pattered into the basket and the sun sank low behind the trees. 'I never scrape the scales from an adder,' she once heard Miss Price say earnestly. 'It takes force from any spell except those in which hemlock is combined with fennel. The only time I ever scrape the scales from an adder is in spells against St Vitus's dance, then for some reason, it gives better results . . .' Sometimes, when Emelius had been speaking, Miss Price would exclaim rather scornfully: 'Well, if you want to go back to the wax image and pin school –' and Carey always wondered what the wax image and pin school was, and why Emelius, having graduated, should want to go back there.

One evening Carey overheard a most curious conversation. It began by Miss Price saying brightly:

'Have you ever tried intrasubstantiary-locomotion?'

There was a mystified silence on the part of Emelius. Then he said, rather uncertainly: 'No. At least, not often.'

'It's awfully jolly,' she went on. 'I had a positive craze for it once.' The damsons pattered gently into the basket, and

Carey wondered if Emelius was as curious as she was.

Miss Price gave a little laugh. She sounded almost girlish. 'Of course, as spells go, it's child's play. But sometimes the easiest things are the most effective, don't you think?'

Emelius cleared his throat. 'I'm not sure that I haven't got it a little muddled in my mind,' he ventured guardedly. 'I may be confusing it with –'

Miss Price laughed quite gaily. 'Oh, you couldn't confuse intrasubstantiary-locomotion with anything else.' She seemed amused.

'No,' admitted Emelius. 'No. I suppose you couldn't.'

'Unless,' said Miss Price, suddenly thoughtful, leaning forward on the rake and gazing earnestly into the middle distance, 'you mean –'

'Yes,' put in Emelius hastily, 'that's what I do mean.'

'What?' asked Miss Price wonderingly.

'That's what I was confusing it with.'

'With what?'

'With –' Emelius hesitated. 'With what you were going to say.'

'But intrasubstantiary-locomotion is *quite* different.' Miss Price sounded surprised and rather puzzled.

'Oh yes,' admitted Emelius hastily, 'it's completely different, but all the same – '

'You see intrasubstantiary-locomotion is making a pair of shoes walk without any feet in them.'

'Ah yes,' agreed Emelius, with relief. '*Shoes*. That's it.'

'Or a suit of clothes get up and sit down.'

'Yes,' said Emelius, but he sounded a little less sure of himself.

'Of course,' went on Miss Price enthusiastically, 'the very best results are got from washing on a line.' She laughed delightedly. 'It's amazing what you can do with washing on a line.'

'Astounding,' agreed Emelius. He gave a nervous little laugh.

'Except sheets,' Miss Price pointed out.

'Oh, sheets are no good.'

'It has to be wearing apparel. Something you can make look as if a person was inside it.'

'Naturally,' said Emelius, rather coldly.

At first Miss Price, anxious not to have him on her hands for too long, had taken great trouble to explain the circumstances which governed the length of Emelius's visit, but, latterly, as he began to settle down and find happiness in the discovery of friends, she too seemed sad at the thought of his departure. And contented as he was, he himself was a little worried about the Fire of London, and what might have happened to his rooms in Cripplegate and, also, he felt in duty bound (having read of his aunt's death in the churchyard) to attend to the business of inheriting her estate. 'I can always come back and visit you,' he would explain, 'if you could come and fetch me.'

But Miss Price didn't approve of this idea. 'One thing or another,' she would say, 'not this dashing about between centuries. A settled life is good for everyone. I think the wise thing to do would be to give up your London establishment and settle down in your aunt's house at Pepperinge Eye. And we could walk up there sometimes, and it would be nice to think of your living there. You would not seem so far away.'

Emelius thought this over. 'It's a good piece of land,' he said at last, but he spoke rather sadly.

Carey, who was present, said warmly, as if to comfort him: 'We'd go there often. We'd sit on the stones in the parlour, near where the fire-place was, and we'd feel awfully near you –'

Emelius looked at her. 'I'd like you to see the house,' he said. 'As it is in my day.'

Carey turned to Miss Price.

'Couldn't we go just once?' she asked.

Miss Price tightened her lips. 'It's always "just once," Carey. You've had your "just once" and we've still to take Mr Jones back.'

'If we promise not to stay a minute, just a second, when we take him back, couldn't we just go once and see him at his aunt's house?'

Emelius glanced at Miss Price's face, then sadly down at the lawn.

'It isn't,' said Miss Price uncomfortably, 'that I wouldn't be happy to go and see Mr Jones, especially in that dear little house, but –'

'But what?' asked Carey.

'I'm responsible for you children. There seems to be no way of knowing what may happen on these outings –'

'Well,' said Carey reasonably, 'it's hardly much of any outing – just to go and visit Mr Jones – in his quiet little house. At Pepperinge Eye – not two miles away.'

'I know, Carey,' Miss Price pointed out. 'But what about that quiet day we planned on the beach?'

'Well, after all, that was a cannibal island. This is quite different. Mr Jones's aunt's dear little house. At Pepperinge Eye –'

'If you came just once,' said Emelius. 'Say, a week after I left, just to see it all. Then after that you could just come in spirit –'

'In spirit?' said Miss Price dubiously.

'I mean just take a walk up to where the house was and

we'll think of each other,' said Emelius.

Miss Price sat silent. They could not read her expression. At last she said, rather surprisingly: 'I don't like flying in the face of nature —'

'Well,' Carey pointed out, 'isn't the broomstick — ?'

'No,' said Miss Price, 'that's different. That's accepted — witches have always flown on broomsticks.' She paused. 'No, I don't quite know how to put it, and I don't really like to mention it, but there's no getting away from the fact that, as far as we're concerned, Mr Jones is long since dead and buried.'

Emelius stared glumly at the grass between his feet. He could not deny it.

'I don't hold it against him,' went on Miss Price. 'We must all come to it sooner or later, but it doesn't seem wise or natural to foster these attachments with one who is no more.'

They sat silent; then, after a bit, Emelius sighed. 'There is no record of my death in the churchyard,' he pointed out.

Miss Price pursed up her lips. 'That proves nothing. We did not look in the annexe behind the yew hedge.'

'Don't let's,' said Carey suddenly.

A CHANGE OF MIND

*B*ut Miss Price stuck to the original plan. When Emelius's clothes arrived from the cleaners they took him back. They dropped him in Goat Alley at night, and did not stay a minute. Miss Price never liked long drawn-out goodbyes, and in her efforts to spare everybody's feelings she was almost too businesslike. She would not 'step upstairs' to try his cherry cordial. She bundled the children back on to the bed with almost indecent haste, and left Emelius standing, sombre and dark-robed, in the moonlit street. Embarrassed she seemed, and worried by the whole business, and she was sharp with the children when they got home, and next day flung herself into bottling as though she tried to drown the memory of that sad white face deep in sliced apricot and squashed tomato pulp. She did not join the children on their expeditions, and the bed-knob had been hidden away.

The happy atmosphere of the little house seemed to have dispersed, and the children wandered into the fields and sat on gates, talking and kicking their heels. They chewed long stalks of grass and quarrelled idly, while the end of the holidays loomed in sight and lowered over them.

No one even mentioned Emelius until one day at tea when Miss Price, quite suddenly, brought the subject up herself.

'I wonder,' she said, gazing pensively at the brown teapot, 'if we should have taken Mr Jones right home.'

The atmosphere at once became electric. Carey laid down her teaspoon. All three pairs of eyes were fixed on Miss Price's face.

'But we did,' said Charles, after a moment.

'I mean,' went on Miss Price, 'leaving him in the street like that. It was rather rude.'

'Yes,' said Carey. 'His house might have been damaged in the fire, or anything. He might have had nowhere to sleep that night.'

Miss Price looked worried. 'It was just that we agreed, didn't we? – not to stay.'

'Yes,' said Carey. 'You remember we asked you whether if we promised not to stay a minute, a second, when we took him back you would let us go later and visit him properly.'

'I didn't promise anything,' replied Miss Price hastily. She poured herself out another cup of tea. As she stirred it she said uncertainly: 'But I think he's all right, don't you? He could always go down to Pepperinge Eye.'

'Yes,' said Carey, 'I'm sure he'd manage.'

'And yet,' went on Miss Price, 'in some ways Mr Jones is rather helpless. That fire, you know, they say there were riots afterwards.' Miss Price, without noticing what she was doing, put another spoonful of sugar in her tea.

'If one could write to him . . .' she suggested.

'Yes,' said Carey, 'but we can't.'

Charles cleared his throat. 'Would you like Paul and me just to run down and take a look at him?'

Carey opened her mouth. 'Without me?' she said indignantly.

'No, no,' put in Miss Price. 'It wouldn't be fair to leave Carey. Perhaps,' she hesitated, 'perhaps we ought *all* to go.'

The children were silent. They dared not urge her. Carey crossed her thumbs and stared fixedly at the tablecloth.

'We could just go to his lodgings and peep in at the window. Just to see if he's all right, don't you know. We wouldn't disturb him. I think,' said Miss Price, 'it would be *kind.*'

The children did not speak.

'Once we knew he was all right,' went on Miss Price, 'we could come back and settle down happily to our lives.'

'Yes,' said Carey guardedly.

'Don't you think?' asked Miss Price.

'Oh yes,' said Charles.

'Although this is a flying visit,' said Miss Price, 'I think we should be prepared for any emergency.' She took down her father's sword from its hook on the wall, and tested the blade with her finger. Then she strapped the scabbard to the bed-rail. Carey and Charles were folding blankets, and Paul was opening out the groundsheet. It was nine o'clock in the morning, and they were all gathered together in Miss Price's bedroom to prepare for the journey.

'You see,' went on Miss Price, 'although I'm now convinced it is our duty to go, it is a great responsibility for me, now, at the end of the holidays. I don't feel justified in taking risks. I'm not sure that we shouldn't be disguised –'

'How do you mean?' asked Charles.

'We look so very twentieth century,' said Miss Price. 'And it will be daylight this time.'

'I know!' exclaimed Carey. 'Let's hire something from a

costumier, like we did for the school play.'

'No, no,' said Miss Price. 'I couldn't go in fancy dress. I shouldn't feel myself at all – but I have that black cloak and you children would be all right in long dressing-gowns, pinned up at the neck.'

'Oh, Miss Price, that wouldn't look like *anything*. The

costumier would have the exact dress. I have seven and sixpence.'

'It would cost more than seven and sixpence,' said Miss Price. 'And we're only going to stay ten minutes. Dressing-gowns are good enough. You are always apt to overdo things, Carey, and become fantastic. Now help me turn the mattress.'

'I should think,' said Carey, taking hold of the mattress, 'we should look jolly fantastic walking about London in Charles II's reign wearing twentieth-century dressing-gowns pinned up at the neck –'

'Now, Carey, that's enough. I have not the remotest intention of walking about London, and you're very lucky to be going at all.'

*E*melius opened his eyes. Then he closed them again.
The light hurt them. 'It is a dream,' he told himself,
'a nightmare, the worst I have ever had.' He felt
cold, but too bruised and tired to mind that he felt cold. He
just lay there, on the stone floor, trying not to wake up. But,
after a while, his eyes seemed to open of their own accord,
and he saw the small, barred window, and the grey sky
beyond. He sat up suddenly, and then cried out with pain as
the movement hurt him. He smelt the wetness of his clothes,
and his hands slipped on the floor. Slowly he began to
remember: yesterday, the horse-pond; today, the stake. . .

He had been betrayed. During the Fire of London men
had lost their heads. A papist plot, they said, had caused it,
and Frenchmen had thrown fireballs to burn the city.
Somebody had spoken of Emelius, who lived so mysterious-
ly in his dim lodging off Goat Alley, and king's men had
searched his dwelling. There they found evidence of witchcraft and of sorcery and when, on his return, he had walked
up the dark stairway, two men had met him at the head and

another, appearing from nowhere, cut off his retreat at the foot. He had been thrown into prison and tried, so angry were the people, almost immediately. When it was proved that he was no Frenchman, nor implicated in any 'papist' plot, they accused him of having helped to cause the fire by magic. It was strange, they said, how he had left the city just before and returned when danger was over, and that his house, in the midst of such destruction, was barely touched.

Ah, the horse-pond . . . that was terror! One little boy he remembered, a little boy with bare feet, who had run along beside him, ahead of the crowd, as they half dragged, half carried him towards the pond; a little brown-faced boy, who shouted and jeered, showing his white teeth, and who stopped every few moments to pick a stone out of the dust. Emelius would try to duck, to shy away from that stone when it came singing through the air. He felt the little boy's laughing delighted face as part of the pain when the stone cut his cheek or glanced off his head.

And the tying of his hands and feet, the constable standing by, the clergyman's solemn face. And then the sickening plunge downwards to the green water, the floating duck-weed . . . a little parchment boat, half soaked, caught on a twig . . . and then the choking, greenish darkness . . . a noise in his ears like a scale played quickly on a violin. If he sank and died there in the water, it showed he was a human man and innocent of magic, but if he lived, that was a sign that he lived by supernatural powers, and they would burn him at the stake.

Then up he had come, choking, spluttering, coughing. The thick robe, tied at the ankles, had held the air. He saw the sunlight, and heard the frightened quack of ducks. Then down, down again, into the water . . . the singing in his ears, the blackness; a blackness which thickened and spread, calming his fear, blotting out his thoughts.

And now it was morning. He had lain all night where they had thrown him on the cold floor. Cold . . . yes, he was cold, right through to the kernel of his heart, but he would not be cold for long; soon his wet clothes would steam; he would feel the hot steam rise upwards past his face, and then his clothes would smoulder; he would feel the heat of their smouldering against his skin, and their dry smoke in his nostrils – then, suddenly, the clothes would flare up into a running flame . . .

The stake . . . it was years since they had burned anyone at the stake. Witches and sorcerers were hanged nowadays, not burned. It was barbarous, monstrous, to burn a man alive! But the people were obsessed today by fire, fire, fire. . . .

'Oh,' cried Emelius, putting his hands on his closed eye-lids. 'The stake . . . the stake . . . save me from the stake!'

He sat quiet, his face hidden in his hands, as though, if he were still enough, he might find that, after all, he had died there in the horse-pond, and it was all over. 'Here I am,' he thought bitterly, 'condemned for witchcraft, and I never knew a spell that worked.'

If it had been Miss Price – that would have been fairer, she was a witch, a real one, but no one would dare burn her. No one would pull Miss Price out of her tidy little house and drag her down the High Street to the village green. If she paid her taxes, observed the English Sunday, and worked for the Red Cross, no one bothered what she did with the rest of her time. She could create a black cat as big as an elephant, and no one would molest her as long as she kept it off other people's property and did not ill-treat it.

'Oh, Miss Price, if you knew –' groaned Emelius, his eyes

hidden. 'If you knew that I am to be burned at the stake!'

'I do know,' said a voice. 'They told me at your lodging.'

Emelius slowly drew his fingers from his eyes. He stared round the cell. It was empty.

His fear, perhaps, was turning him crazy. The voice had seemed real, not very loud, and quite matter-of-fact. And then he saw her – a face at the window, and two hands with whitened knuckles grasping the bars. The face stared at him from under a black cowl and, at first, he did not recognize the shadowed eye sockets and the lips compressed with effort, but then the long nose leapt, as it were, into his fear-dimmed vision, a pink-tipped banner of indignation and righteous wrath.

'Such a time getting here,' she complained testily. 'Asking, asking. And such rudeness.'

Still Emelius did not speak. He was shivering as if, suddenly, he had come alive to the cold.

'Not a soul that seems to understand the king's English,' went on the angry voice. She was panting slightly as if she held herself up by her own efforts. 'I don't see how you've stood it. And the dirt, the untidiness, the smells . . . but we won't go into that now –' She slipped out of sight with a sharp exclamation. Then, after a moment, she appeared again. 'Lost my foothold,' she explained. 'I'm in a very awkward position. But you're locked in and there's no room for the bed.'

Emelius moistened his lips with his tongue. His eyes were fixed on the face at the window.

'They swam me in the horse-pond,' he moaned, as if he were talking to himself. 'In the horse-pond –'

'Well, never mind,' said Miss Price briskly. 'Don't dwell on it!' She looked down and Emelius heard her say indistinctly: 'Well, move your finger, Carey. It's your own fault. I didn't mean to tread on it.' There was a pause, then he heard Miss Price say: 'Yes, he's all right. Very wet. But the cell's too small for the bed.' She peered in at him. 'Just a minute,' she said, and disappeared.

He heard the gentle sound of voices. He lay back. Thankfulness crept up from his toes, up and up, until his heart swelled from it, and it forced tears from his eyes; hot painful tears that squeezed out from between his closed lids. Miss Price was here. She would save him. Miss Price never undertook a thing she did not finish, and Miss Price did everything so well.

After a while she appeared again. 'Now,' she said, 'you must pull yourself together. We're not going to let you be burned, but we can't stay here. It's broad daylight, and I'm standing on the bed-rail –'

'Don't go!' begged Emelius.

'I must go, for the moment, and find a place for the bed. There's going to be a storm. And it was such nice weather when we left home.'

'What shall I do?' gasped Emelius.

'There's nothing for you to do at the moment, and there are two men at the main door playing dice. You must keep calm and try not to fuss.' She looked at him speculatively. 'Tidy yourself up a bit and you'll feel better.' Then, once more, she disappeared.

This time she did not come back and, after a while, Emelius, because Miss Price had told him to, began picking long strands of green slime off his fur-trimmed robe. He found a water-beetle up his sleeve, and his shoes were full of mud. Yes, she would save him, but how? It was not going to be easy. The barred window, sunk deep in the wall, was only a foot square, and the locked door was made of iron.

'She's an awful long time coming,' said Carey.

The three children sat on the bed in a disused cow-byre. The ground was trodden and dusty, and a pile of greyish hay rotted in the corner. Through the broken door they could see a bleak field below a dark and lowering sky. It was a dismal place but, as Miss Price had pointed out, a secluded one, in which to hide the bed. She had gone off, wrapped in her black cloak, broomstick in one hand and sword in the other, to see what could be done for Emelius.

'She's been gone an hour, about,' said Charles, walking to the door. The dark sky had a whitish streak in it, which shed an unreal, livid light on the trees and hedges. There was a sudden quivering brightness. Charles dodged back as a rumbling arch of thunder unrolled itself above the roof. 'It startled me,' he said.

'Do you think we ought to go and look for her?' asked Carey.

'What about the bed? Someone ought to stay and watch

it.'

'Nobody will come here,' said Carey. 'They're all gone to the burning. I think that we ought all to go or *all* to stay. Not split up.'

Charles looked thoughtfully across the field towards the gate which led into the road. 'Let's all go then,' he said.

At the doorway Carey glanced back at the bed. It stood incongruously bright, with its legs sunk deep in dust and broken straw. 'I wonder if we shall see it again,' she thought to herself. 'I wonder what we are letting ourselves in for.'

As they walked along, in the gloomy light, between the uneven houses and their deserted gardens, they looked around them curiously. It was not very different from parts of England they knew. New houses squatted beside old ones. An inn sign creaked in a sudden gust of wind, but the inn was deserted. Everyone had gone to the burning.

'Smithfield,' said Charles, 'where the meat market is. It's really part of London, but it looks like country.'

Horses and carts were tethered to posts. There were a great many half-starved cats about and rough-coated, mangy-looking dogs, which ran slyly down the alleyways, but there were no people. Old bones and rags and broken pan-lids in the gutters, and there was a strong smell of tanning. As they walked they began to hear the murmur of a crowd.

'Look!' said Carey in a low voice.

A richly dressed man was leading a horse out of a stable yard. He wore leather boots or leggings, which came up to his thighs, and a skirted coat. Lace fell over his wrists as far as his knuckle bones, and a great dark wig moved heavily on his shoulders. As they came abreast of him they smelt his perfume, a strange, rich, spicy smell, which mingled oddly with the stench of the tannery. Preparing to mount he stared at them wonderingly. His pale face was full of disapproval. Carey nervously put up her hand to cover her safety-pin, but he was not looking at their clothes. Something deeper seemed to worry him. 'A poor wretch burned at the stake,' he said as they passed close beside him, 'a fine sight for children!'

Carey stared back at him with frightened eyes. She felt as you always feel when a complete stranger speaks to you angrily. As the clatter of his hoofs died away behind them, the children walked in silence. They felt guilty, as if it were their fault that Emelius was to be burned alive.

Then suddenly the road opened into a square, or green, and they came upon the crowd. It was like a painting Carey had seen somewhere, or like an historical film; except it was more colourful than a painting and dirtier than an historical film. Boys had climbed trees and railings; every window was full of people. Above the babble of talk certain voices were heard calling some indistinct, monotonous phrase. Carey jumped when just behind her a woman yodelled:

'Fair lemons and oranges.
Oranges and citrons.'

They could get in no closer. They were jammed close beside a fat woman with three children, and what seemed to be the railing of a cattle pen. The fat woman, who wore a white cap round her red face, with a hat on top of it, was breaking a cake for her children. It smelt of cinnamon and made Carey feel hungry.

Carey put her foot on the bottom rail of the cattle pen and pushed herself up between the knees of the boys who sat on top of it. Ah, now she could see the stake! It was raised only a little above the crowd. Two men with muskets slung on their backs were busy with ropes. When they moved aside she saw Emelius, a limp sagged figure. He was tied round the chest. She could not see any lower than his knees. She could not see the faggots. There was no sign of Miss Price.

Charles climbed up beside her. She heard him exclaim when he saw Emelius, and then Paul was pulling at the skirt of her dressing-gown.

'Could I have a toffee apple?' he said.

Carey stepped down. Paul was too young to see Emelius burn, or even be told about it. 'We haven't any money, Paul,' Carey explained kindly, 'to buy toffee apples,' but she looked round and there indeed was a woman with a tray slung round her neck selling toffee apples right and left – toffee apples and lollipops on sticks. The woman with the three children gave Paul a piece of cinnamon cake. She stared at them curiously. 'She notices our clothes,' thought Carey.

Then a hush fell on the crowd. Someone up near the stake was speaking, but they could not see him, nor hear what he said. 'They're going to start soon,' announced Charles from his perch on the railings. Carey saw a thin trail of smoke. She climbed up beside Charles again to see, but it was only a man with a spluttering torch which he held aloft as if waiting for an order. Someone else was speaking now. Carey glimpsed a long form in black, a lawyer, perhaps, or a clergyman.

The figure at the stake still sagged, the head hanging forward on the chest. 'Miss Price . . . Miss Price . . .' breathed Carey, clinging to the rail. 'Save him. Oh please, save poor Emelius.'

The voice finished speaking. The crowd became terribly silent. Other people tried to climb on the railing. All eyes were turned towards the stake. Suddenly there was a roll of drums. The man with the torch circled it about his head, and flung it downwards, in amongst the faggots.

Carey shrieked and jumped down off the railing, hiding her eyes. The roll of drums went on, swelling in intensity. Clouds of smoke rose up against the dark and threatening sky. A quivering flash and, for one livid second, the whole scene stood etched in lightning – lightning which played in forks across the gloomy sky – then the sound of the drums was drowned in a crashing, ear-splitting roll of thunder, roaring and trembling across the heavens until it seemed to shake the very earth on which they stood.

Then Carey heard shrieks and cries. She clambered, pushing for a foothold, upon the railing to see what had happened. Something seemed to be bending the crowd like a field of corn in wind, something of which they seemed afraid. The shrieks of the women shrilled and multiplied. There was a movement of pushing, of fighting, of panic. Carey pulled Paul beside her close against the railing. Paul began to cry.

'Charles,' cried Carey, her voice breaking with excitement. 'Look! Look!'

Something was skimming low over the crowd, a great black bird it seemed, which flew in narrowing circles, and whose passage seemed to cut a swath in the frightened mob as it passed, as hair falls aside from the comb.

'It's she! It's Miss Price!' cried Carey. 'Paul it's Miss Price! Charles . . .'

People were pushing, screaming, rushing to get out of reach. Now, it was coming towards their corner, swooping low and steady on its curving flight. The fat woman shrieked and ran, dragging her children after her. The boys jumped down off the railing. 'A witch, a witch!' they screamed hoarsely. 'A witch on a broomstick!'

But Carey and Charles, holding Paul tight against them, kept their places. They gazed upwards with anxious eyes at the black and fluttering figure which came towards them in the gloom. Shrouded and unrecognizable, it swept past, and an eerie wail, thin and terrifying, trailed behind it on the wind.

People had run away, down the side streets, down the alleys. There were spaces of empty, trodden grass and littered dusty ground. A basket seller was collecting his stock, which rolled around in every direction, but he dropped it all again as the dark figure flew near him and ran 'hell for leather' for the entrance of a tavern.

Now the children could see the stake quite clearly. The smoke had cleared, and red tongues of flame, licking their way upwards through the faggots, shone weirdly in the leaden gloom. Emelius, bound round the chest and ankles, hung forward on his ropes.

'He's catching fire!' shrieked Carey. 'Oh, Miss Price, hurry! hurry!'

Soldiers, who had acted as a cordon against the crowd, formed a group, training their muskets on the broomstick's flight. Only one remained beside the stake, and he seemed to be charging his gun, looking up fearfully from time to time as if he feared the dark swooping figure might come upon him from behind.

'Perhaps she's forgotten,' Charles reminded Carey fearfully. 'She burnt the books.'

There was a report, which echoed back against the houses. One of the soldiers had fired. Once more the lightning flashed, and thunder pealed across the angry sky. The square was empty now, save for the soldiers and the huddled group of children beside the cattle pen. The ground was scattered with litter. Benches, chairs, and stools –

things which people had brought to stand on – lay overturned and broken.

As the flying figure approached the stake the remaining soldier fled to join the others, clutching his musket. The broomstick and the sweeping black cloak seemed almost to touch the burning faggots when the children saw a sword flash.

'It's her father's sword,' exclaimed Charles excitedly. 'She's going to cut him free.'

Carey was reminded, watching the awkward efforts to bring the broomstick within striking distance yet not too close, of a left-handed golfer trying to play polo.

'Oh dear,' she cried, in an agony of fear. 'She'll cut his head off.'

Emelius, aware at last, twisted and leaned and strained at his cords in terrified efforts to escape the deadly thrusts. A gust of spark-filled smoke blew against his face, and the children saw him coughing. Still the attack continued.

'Careful!' shouted Carey. 'Please, oh, please, Miss Price.'

Again there was a report, followed immediately by two others. The soldiers were firing. Carey, glancing fearfully at the bell-mouthed weapons, wondered how such guns could miss.

'They've got her,' said Charles then, in his most reserved voice.

'No,' cried Carey wildly, 'no, they can't have!' Her eyes flew back to the stake, and she covered her mouth quickly to hold back a scream.

The broomstick was poised, motionless, shuddering, above the crackling wood. The sword dropped, and stuck upright, quivering among the faggots. The broomstick wavered and sank downward towards the smoke and flame. Then, as they watched, painfully it seemed to pull itself free. It rose a little and made a limping, hesitating flight towards the head of a road leading out of the square. The soldiers turned slowly, keeping the fluttering object covered with their guns. Figures appeared in doorways. Several men, braver than the others, ventured into the street. All eyes were fixed on the black and tattered object which rose a little and then sank once more towards the ground, in painful hopping flight.

The children no longer watched the stake, where each second for Emelius became uncomfortably warmer; their eyes were fixed on the broomstick. They gripped each other in an agony of fear. Nothing seemed to matter in the world except Miss Price and her safety. As they watched, the broomstick rose a little. Jerkily swaying, rather drunkenly, as if it had lost its sense of direction, it made off down the street, at about the level of the first-floor windows.

Then a man threw a brick, and the soldiers fired again. The broomstick stopped in mid air.

For about the twentieth part of a second the children saw the folds of the black cloak hang limp, before the whole equipage dropped like a stone. Then they could see it no more. People ran out of doorways, out of yards, out of alleys. Some were armed with staves, some with clubs; they saw one man, a butcher he must have been, with a large and shining chopper. All these people made for the spot where the broomstick had fallen. The narrow mouth of the street was choked with an ever-increasing crowd, composed mostly of boys and men. No one glanced at the stake, or felt the sudden onslaught of the rain. It poured down suddenly, a slanting rushing sheet of water, mingling with the tears on Carey's face, and turning the churned dust into mud.

'Miss Price . . . Miss Price . . .' sobbed Carey, while the rain ran down her hair into the neck of her dressing-gown. She hardly noticed Charles had left her side. She did not know how he had got there when she saw him clamber on the steaming faggots, which hissed and blackened under the downpour. She watched Charles seize the sword, and chop at the ropes which bound Emelius. She saw Emelius fall forward on the piled wood, and the wood roll from under him. She saw Emelius hit the ground, and Charles climbing down from the stake, sword in hand. She saw Emelius picking himself up from the ground in a dazed way, his charred robe hanging in strips about his yellow-stockinged legs. She saw Charles urging him, talking to him, pulling

him by the arm. Then Charles and Emelius were there
beside her where she leaned with Paul against the cattle pen.
Charles was pulling off Emelius's coat, so that he stood in
shirt and breeches and wrinkled yellow stockings. . .

'Miss Price, Miss Price . . .' Carey went on sobbing.

'They won't recognize you so easily like that,' Charles
was explaining to Emelius. 'You're not a bit burnt. Lucky
your clothes were so wet. Come, Carey,' he went on, looking
white but determined. 'Do shut up, we've got to get back to
the bed.'

'But Miss Price —' cried Carey wildly. 'We can't leave
Miss Price.'

'We must,' said Charles. 'There's nothing we can do now.
She would want us to be sensible.'

Paul began to bellow loudly. He had no inhibitions. If
Miss Price was dead he was not going to be brave. Paul's
noise had a steadying effect on Carey; she took his hand.
'Quiet, Paul,' she said, sniffing. 'We can cry when we get
home.'

They could not walk quickly because Charles had burned
his feet. Perhaps it was just as well; running might have
aroused suspicion. Emelius seemed in a dream. He did not
speak and gazed before him as if he still saw a black figure
fluttering wildly on a broomstick. As they neared the gate
leading into the field the same fear descended on all of them.
Suppose the bed had gone . . .

Carey and Paul had dropped a little behind, and it was
Charles who entered the cowshed first. When Carey heard
him exclaim, she deliberately stood still – waiting there in
the squishy grass while the rain poured down. She felt she
couldn't bear much more.

'Carey!' Charles was shouting. 'Carey! Come and see!'

Carey dragged herself to the door of the cowshed. At first,

in the gloom, she could see nothing. Then she distinguished the outline of the bed. A figure was lying on it – a figure propped up on one elbow – and a pair of angry eyes met her own in a stare of baleful accusation.

'Oh, Miss Price!' cried Carey. She clutched at the door-post, as if she might have fallen.

'You may well look guilty,' scolded Miss Price. Even in that light the tip of her nose was an angry pink. 'You are the most thoughtless and untrustworthy children. I distinctly told you to stay by the bed. I've been frightened out of my wits about you. Out of my wits. I come back here, worn out with witchcraft, longing to put my feet up for five minutes – and what do I find?'

'Oh!' cried Carey. She rushed across the cowshed. She flung herself upon the bed. She sobbed down Miss Price's neck as if her heart would break.

'There!' said Miss Price uncomfortably, patting Carey's shoulder blades. 'There! No need to get emotional. We've all been a little upset, that's what it is.'

'You're safe,' gasped Carey. 'Darling Miss Price. They didn't kill you.'

Miss Price drew her head away as if she were surprised. 'Kill me?' she exclaimed, with something like horror. She stared at them unbelievingly. 'Gracious goodness alive, you didn't imagine that was me on the broomstick?'

'Then what was it, Miss Price?' asked poor Carey, wiping her eyes. 'Whatever was it?'

Miss Price stared at her a moment longer, then she gave a little triumphant glance in the direction of Emelius. 'That,' she said, blushing slightly, 'was just a particularly apposite use of intrasubstantiary-locomotion.'

But Emelius, stretched out wearily on the hay in the corner, did not even look up.

AND FARTHER STILL

*E*melius was put to bed in Charles's room, and remained there several days. He was suffering, Miss Price said, from 'shock.' Charles's feet were more scorched than burned, and some yellow ointment spread on gauze soon healed them. In a week's time the vacation would be over, and Miss Price was gentler, kinder to them than they had ever known her. She spent her time between packing for the children and arranging trays for Emelius. She was so kind, so unusually long-suffering, that the children were a little afraid. They thought Emelius must be worse than Miss Price had at first supposed. Several times Carey saw a strange man in the house, and it was not always the same one. Once Miss Price came downstairs with two of them at her heels. All three went into the dining-room and closed the door and, for over an hour, the house felt tense with mystery. She seemed, too, to be writing a lot of letters and running off down to the village to telephone. But instead of getting fussed she became kinder and kinder. They didn't like it at all, and were filled with dread when, on the last day of the holidays, she summoned them rather solemnly into the sitting-room where, since Emelius came, Charles had been sleeping.

The three children sat on Charles's bed, and Miss Price, facing them, took a little upright chair. There was a feeling of great tenseness in the air.

Miss Price cleared her throat and clasped her hands together in her lap.

'Children,' she said, 'what I am going to tell you will not come altogether as a surprise. You have noticed a good deal of coming and going in the house during this past week, and must have gathered something was afoot.'

Miss Price moistened her lips with her tongue and clasped her hands a little tighter together. The children's eyes watched every movement, seeking some hint of what was going to come.

'I do not possess anything of great value,' went on Miss Price, 'but my belongings, such as they are, are in excellent repair. The kitchen sink, put in only last year, cost me, with the labour, close on fifty pounds, but I shall not leave the bathroom fittings. It was a help to me, in making my decision, to remember that I could take these with me. If I have a weakness, and we all have many, it is a weakness for modern plumbing. I've nothing against the Simple Life, assuming that there is such a thing, but bathing in a wash-tub is so unnecessarily complicated.' Miss Price paused. 'The proceeds will go to the Red Cross,' she added.

Carey leaned forward. She seemed to hesitate a moment, and then she said, 'What proceeds, Miss Price?'

'I keep telling you, Carey. The proceeds from the sale of the house.'

'You're going to sell the house!'

'Carey, try to pay more attention when people are

speaking to you. I'm selling the house and the furniture, except, as I say, the bathroom fitments.'

'And you're giving the money to the Red Cross?'

'Every penny.'

'Why?' asked Charles.

'To compensate this century for the loss of an able-bodied woman.'

Carey began to smile. She half stood up and then sat down again. 'I see,' she said slowly. 'Oh, Miss Price –'

'I don't see,' complained Charles.

'Charles,' said Carey, turning to him eagerly. 'It's sort of good and bad news. Miss Price means –' She looked at Miss Price uncertainly. 'I think Miss Price means –'

Miss Price made her face quite expressionless. She cleared her throat. 'Perhaps I didn't make it quite clear, Charles,' she conceded, 'that Mr Jones has asked me to share his life.' She allowed Charles a small and dignified smile. 'And I have accepted.'

Charles stared. He looked completely bewildered. 'You're going to live in the seventeenth century?'

'Of necessity,' said Miss Price. 'Mr Jones can't stay here and, there, we have a house and live-stock, an orchard – and Mr Jones has a little something laid by.'

'But how will you go?' asked Charles. 'Unless Paul comes too?'

'It's all arranged. Mr Bisselthwaite will call for you tomorrow morning, and will put you on the train. And this evening, after supper, Paul will stand on the floor near the head of the bed, and twist the knob.'

'You're going tonight?' exclaimed Charles.

'Unfortunately we must. I dislike doing things in a hurry but, without Paul, we have no means of conveyance.'

Carey turned sideways, so that she lay on one elbow. She

picked some fluff off the blanket, staring closely at her hand.

'Miss Price –' she said.

'Well?'

'Will you –' Carey stared hard at the blanket. 'Will you like it?'

Miss Price lifted her hands and let them fall on the arms of the chair. Strangely enough she did not, as Carey expected, have an answer ready.

'Mr Jones and I,' said Miss Price slowly, gazing at the wall as if she could see through it, 'are two lonely people. We shall be better together.'

'The bed can never come back,' said Charles.

Miss Price, gazing at the wall, did not reply.

Once again there was a faint film of dust (and two feathers) where the bed had stood. But this time the room looked barer still, with the rugs rolled up and the dressing-table drawers left slightly open. A crumpled piece of tissue flew lightly across the room and caught itself against the leg of the washstand.

She had gone. Where a minute before there had been bustle and flurry, tyings-up and tuckings-in, hurried good-byes and last-minute hugs, there was silence and emptiness.

The bed had been dangerously overloaded. The bathroom plumbing, dissected amateurishly by Charles and Emelius, and wrapped in ironing blankets and dust sheets, took up so much room to start with. And then, besides the clothes-basket and two suit-cases, there were the last-minute things which Miss Price could not bear to leave behind. The silver cream jug, her extra hot-water bottle, an egg beater, a cake tin tied with string, in which she had put her store of tea, some biscuits, a packet of Ryvita, and six tins of sardines. There were her apostle spoons and the best tea-cloth, her father's sword, her photographs, a bottle of lavender water . . . They had tied and retied it all with the clothes line but, all the same, it looked terribly perilous, with Miss Price and Emelius perched on top. In spite of everything, Carey pointed out, Miss Price would wear her best straw hat, which had been 'done over' by a woman in the village. 'Better to wear it than pack it,' she had insisted, as if there had been no other alternative. She had cried a little when she said goodbye to the children, and reminded them that Mrs Kithatten down the road was coming in to cook their breakfast; and that their tickets were on the mantelpiece in the dining-room; and that Mr Bisselthwaite would be there by nine-thirty; and to remind Mrs Kithatten that the men would be along any time after one to check the inventory; and that they were to boil up the rest of the milk in case it turned before morning.

And then Paul had wished, standing there beside the bed-head and, suddenly, the room was empty, except for the rustling tissue paper and the curtains falling softly back in place as if there had been a wind.

They felt terribly alone. They went downstairs, and the emptiness of the house seemed to follow them. They walked through the kitchen into the scullery. The drying board was still damp from the washing up of the supper things, a washing up Miss Price had shared. The door of the garden stood open and they wandered out. There, by the dustbin, stood a pile of Miss Price's old shoes. One pair, very stiff and mud-caked, were the ones she kept for gardening in wet weather.

The sun was sinking behind the wood, but the hillside was bathed in golden light.

'They'll be there by now,' Charles said at last, breaking the dreary silence.

Carey looked across the shadowed wood to the familiar, friendly slope of Tinker's Hill.

'I know what,' she exclaimed suddenly. 'Let's run up there! We'll be back before dark.'

'Well, we wouldn't see them or anything,' objected Charles.

'It doesn't matter. Miss Price might sort of know.'

It was good to run and climb panting up the sandy paths, through the bracken, on to the turf. It was good to reach the wind and feel the sunshine as, rich and warm, it fell on their shoulders, and sent long shadows bobbing on ahead across the grass.

When they reached the ruined house Carey climbed alone to the highest spot on the wall. She sat with her chin in her hands, as if in a trance, while the wind blew the wisps of hair on her forehead and her motionless shadow stretched out across the blackberry bushes and up the sundrenched hill. Charles and Paul just messed about among the stones, uneasily picking an occasional blackberry and watching Carey.

After a while Carey climbed down. She did not speak. She walked slowly past the boys. There was a far-away expression on her face, and her eyes were dreamy.

'I can see them,' she said in a chanting kind of voice. She stood quite still, among the brambles of the 'apple orchard.'

'Oh, come on, Carey,' said Charles. He knew she was acting but all the same he did not like it.

'I can see them quite plainly,' went on Carey, as if she had not heard. She stretched out her hands in a 'hushing' gesture and raised her face a little, like a picture they had at home called 'The Prophetess.' 'They are walking slowly down the path, hand in hand.' She paused. 'Now, they have stopped under the apple-tree. Miss Price has no hat on. Now they have turned and are looking back at the house –'

'Oh, Carey, come on,' said Charles uncomfortably. 'It's getting dark.'

'Now,' Carey dropped her voice respectfully, 'Mr Jones has kissed Miss Price on the cheek. He's saying –' Carey paused, as if thinking up the words. 'He is saying,' she went on triumphantly: ' "My own true love" . . .'

Then suddenly Charles and Paul saw Carey's expression change. Her eyes widened and her mouth dropped open. She looked round hurriedly, then she ran, almost leapt out of the brambles, and clambered awkwardly upon the wall. She stared downwards at the spot where she had stood.

'What's the matter, Carey? What happened?' cried Charles.

Carey's face was pale. She looked unnerved, but somewhere about her mouth was the shadow of a smile.

'Didn't you hear?' she asked.

'No,' said Charles, 'I didn't hear anything.'

'Didn't you hear Miss Price?'

'*Really* Miss Price!'

'Yes. It was her voice. Quite loud and distinct.'

Charles and Paul looked grave.

'What – what did she say?' stammered Charles.

'She said: "Carey, come at once out of those lettuces." '